EASY FREEDOM

Cathy Harlow, a brilliant young painter, has at last given in to the pressures around her and agreed to marry rock musician superstar, Paul Devlin, and to keep his baby.

But Cathy is still filled with doubts, for her art is the most important thing in her life and at only seventeen she desperately fears being overwhelmed by Dev and his fame and money. Her relationship with Dev has inflicted wounds, which she can't forgive or forget. She feels threatened too, by Dev's best friend Chris, who sees Cathy and Dev and himself, as bound in a kind of mystical triangle.

Cathy's struggle to overcome the stresses of her new life and her attempts to find herself and regain her lost freedom makes an unusual and compelling love story that leads to a moving climax.

Set in the vivid worlds of rock music and art, it is a gripping story about redemption and forgiveness, and also has much to say about the real problems faced by a girl with a vocation.

Liz Berry lives in London. She is a painter who exhibits her work regularly. She has been head of art in an East London high school, a careers guidance counsellor helping young people plan for their futures, worked in politics, and for a well-known examination body. She also runs her own small art gallery.

EASY FREEDOM

Other books by Liz Berry

JANEY AND THE BAND
SING THE BLUES, JANEY
BRIGHT LIGHTS SHINING
FOOL'S GOLD
EASY CONNECTIONS
EASY FREEDOM
MEL
THE CHINA GARDEN
FINDER

CIRCLES OF BECOMING
 (poetry and autobiography)

Website: www.lizberrybooks.com

EASY FREEDOM

Liz Berry

Gallery 41 Books
London

First published 1985 by Victor Gollancz, London
First paperback (signed) edition 2001 Gallery 41Books, London
Revised new edition 2005
Gallery 41Books
3 Church End,
London E17 9RJ
books@gallery41.co.uk

ISBN 978-0-954-88641-7
ISBN 0-9548864-1-0

This is a work of fiction.   Except for the famous bands
mentioned briefly by name in the text, all incidents and
characters in this story, including the bands Easy Connection
and Night Mission, are entirely invented and imaginary.

Printed by
Antony Rowe Limited,
2 Whittle Drive,
Highfield Industrial Estate,
Eastbourne,
East Sussex, BN236QT

Chapter One

'Get ready for the wedding presents,' said Chris Carter, coming into the kitchen of the shabby flat in Hamilton Square, which Cathy Harlow shared with four other students at the London College of Art. He dropped the morning papers on to the kitchen table in front of her, leaned over, his arms rigid on the table edge, smiling down into her eyes. 'Happy ever after,' he said and kissed the tip of her nose.

Cathy moved out of range, her colour rising, and looked down.

The Mirror had scooped the field. The whole of the front page was taken up by a picture. A very romantic picture. Dev, with his arms around her, under the tall ghostly trees of the Square outside. She was standing on tiptoe, kissing him. Winter sunlight, filtering through the branches had split into shards like a misty star above them.

'Happy Ever After,' said the caption. *'Paul Devlin, millionaire megastar and lead guitarist of Easy Connections, whose current album is Number One in the charts on both sides of the Atlantic, is to marry student artist, Cathy Harlow, 17, after all. The on-off stormy romance which hit the headlines...'*

She pushed the paper away. She had not realised, when she agreed to marry Dev yesterday, that the news would get out quite so quickly, or with so much publicity.

The kitchen was full of people and they all seemed to be watching her, waiting for her reaction. Her flat mates Julie Ellis, making coffee, and Nick Howard, her ex-boyfriend, frying bacon for them all, at the cooker, Chris Carter.

Dev, across the table, was watching her too, covertly. He stretched out his legs luxuriously and folded his arms behind his long dark-gold hair, but his eyes, under half-closed, lazy lids, were watchful and intense. He had spent the night on the lumpy sofa in the communal lounge. He was used to sleeping in odd places and it hadn't worried him. This morning he looked disturbingly alive, burning with energy.

He was still wearing the tight satin trousers and shirt he had worn to his gig the previous night, and not much else, Cathy thought. The shirt hung open, unbuttoned, revealing his muscular body, bare to the hips, and the carved pendant he often wore.

He read Cathy's look instantly. He tilted his chair back, lifting his hips and opening his thighs invitingly. Cathy turned her head, blushing furiously and Dev exchanged grins with Chris.

'Coffee,' said Julie, putting a cup in front of Cathy. She looked over her shoulder at the paper. 'Wow! Film Star stuff.'

Cathy laughed. 'Monty Python? I didn't see a photographer. A telephoto lens I suppose. I feel like a goldfish.'

'Slim and gold with sexy undulations,' said Chris, and they all laughed.

Julie was doing her best not to look at Chris Carter, knowing her knees would feel weak and her stomach like water. The lead singer of Easy Connections had that effect on most girls. It still seemed incredible to Julie that the two famous rock musicians, international stars of the most notorious, exciting, scandalous band in three continents, should actually be *here*, in the old London flat, relaxed and casually at home. She knew that Nick felt the same. He was a fanatical Easy Connections addict, who could recite their total discography with dates, without a check.

Chris Carter was sitting on the kitchen worktop, dangling his washed-out Levis and dirty trainers against the cupboard doors; his jacket was a fine supple leather and he was wearing an identity bracelet of heavy gold. Apart from his amazing good looks, beauty almost, with the high cheek bones, pale hair and grey, almost luminous eyes, Chris shared with Dev a strange magnetic aura, a blend of recklessness, danger, star quality, and maybe, fame.

Chris unzipped his jacket and smiled at Julie. 'Can you spare any of that bacon? I'm starving.'

He was exactly aware of the effect he was having on Julie, Cathy thought, disgusted. Dev and Chris had nothing at all to learn about exploiting their sexuality. They used it quite ruthlessly. But even though you knew that, it didn't make any difference. It was still impossible to ignore either of them.

'I could use a bath,' Dev said.

'Go home then,' Cathy said. 'Plenty of baths there. With gold taps.'

Dev raised an eyebrow, amused. 'You got something against gold taps?'

'No one asked you to stay.'

'I'm not letting you out of my sight until the wedding. This is a shotgun marriage, remember? The shotgun is on *you*. What's wrong with the bath here?'

'Nothing,' said Nick, dishing up the bacon. 'A bit grimy round the edges, maybe, if Bernard used it. Feel free.'

'Thanks,' said Dev. 'Hey, Chris, remember that sauna in Finland with the seventeen-stone female?'

'Yeah. An Experience. But not as good as the pull-up in Nebraska with a tin can on a rope under a tree.' They laughed.

'Cathy, do you want any of this fried bread?' asked Nick.

Cathy swallowed and took a deep breath. 'No thanks.'

Dev looked at her sharply. 'What's the matter?'

'Our little Mama's not feeling too good,' Chris groaned, mock solicitous. His light eyes moved over her body slowly and Cathy flushed again.

Dev swung his chair down and was on his feet in one swift movement. He switched on the electric kettle. 'Tea. Where do you keep it?'

'It's all right,' said Julie. 'I'll make it. I didn't realise Cathy had morning sickness.' She felt upset and uncomfortable about the way Chris had looked at Cathy. 'There's no need...'

But Dev had already found the box of tea bags and was pouring water and milk into a cup. 'Drink the tea, Cathy. Eat a couple of biscuits.'

'I don't want...'

'Drink it.'

Cathy set her teeth, but she sat at the table obediently and drank the tea, as Alun Owen, another of the flat mates, came into the kitchen, trying to close his bulging portfolio.

'Friends, it's later than you think. Ah! The Children of Anwyd! The Lords of the Tylwyth Teg themselves. I felt the vibes boys, I felt the vibes!'

Dev was amused. He raised his arm in graceful salute. 'Gandalf lives, Man!'

'Yeah,' said Chris, sourly. 'It's not the first time we've been called fairies.'

There was an awkward silence. Nick put a plate of bacon into his hand. 'Gods and heroes, you said, last time,' he reminded Alun, carefully.

'Right,' said Alun, 'Tuatha de Danann. The Shining Ones. Gwyn ap Nudd...'

'Chris, I think we've fallen into a den of fans.'

'Not all of them,' said Chris, watching Cathy, who was sitting, deaf to the conversation, staring into space.

'But you know, Cathy is one of the Children too,' Alun said, gently.

She looked like it, too, this morning, thought Julie, with her dark violet-grey eyes and her silky gold hair curling round her shoulders, not pinned up as usual.

For a moment they all stared at her until Cathy became aware of the sudden silence. She looked up and smiled. 'Sorry, did I miss something?'

Chris said sharply to Alun, 'I'm into Taoism and Tantra, not mythology.'

'*Hsien*, then. Reincarnation. Karma.'

Chris stared at him, unusually pale.

Dev said, curiously, 'Hsien?'

'Legendary immortals. Magicians and healers upon whom ordinary mortals project their deepest hopes.'

Dev grinned. 'Sounds okay. Better than fairies anyway.'

'By, that coffee was hot! I've burned my tongue – or bitten it!' Alun pretended to mop his forehead and picked up his portfolio. At the door he gave a clenched fist salute. 'Defend the Four Freedoms, Tongchi!' And went out, cackling with laughter.

'That guy gives me the creeps,' Chris said, irritated.

'Understands too much,' said Dev.

'He did two years in psychology,' offered Julie. 'He doesn't mean anything.'

'He means it. You know who Gwyn ap Nudd is? The God of Death. The Wild Huntsman, who rides a demon horse and hunts men's souls.'

Dev laughed aloud. '*Women's* souls. He must have seen you going over the top at Donington last year, Chris.'

But Chris did not laugh. He had swung his feet up on to the table, trapping Julie between his knees as she passed. He put his arms around her, a question in his eyes.

'I'm late for lectures too, Chris,' Julie said, breathlessly. She knew though, that if he insisted, she would go with him.

He shrugged indifferently and let her go. He picked up another newspaper from the table and began to read aloud with malicious enjoyment a crabby review of someone else's new album.

It was extraordinary how they seemed to take over any place they happened to be, Cathy thought. Even their kitchen did not seem the same any more.

Julie said, impatiently, 'Are you coming, Cathy?'

'Coming where?'

'College, of course. It will be all right now. You'll be able to get in easily. The crowds will have gone.'

Cathy said, her voice wobbling. 'I can't. I'm not allowed. They told me to...' She got up quickly. 'Excuse me, I don't feel well.' The door banged behind her.

'What's the matter? What did I say?'

Chris looked at her blandly. 'The old Col doesn't like scandals.'

Julie's eyes widened. 'You don't mean *they've thrown her out*? But they *can't*! Everybody knows that she's the best painter they've had for years, all the lecturers, *everybody*. Why she's even got that contract with Caleb Crow at the Arundell Gallery. Nobody gets a contract with the Arundell unless they are really fantastic. I don't believe it.'

'Who told you?' Nick asked.

'The horse's mouth, Tom Gibbon.'

'But he's only a Visiting Artist,' Julie said. 'Are you *sure*? It's just incredible.'

'Ask her.'

'But what's she done? She works harder than anybody.'

They watched her with brilliant, mocking eyes.

'She's having a baby,' Dev said. 'Wouldn't get married to the father.'

'*Bad* Paul Devlin...'

'Of *Wicked* Easy Connections.'

'Rock!'

'Booze!'

'Dope!'

'Sex!'

'Endangering the morals of the other students,' Dev and Chris said together and burst out laughing.

'It's not funny!' Julie said, angrily. 'You've got a weird sense of humour.'

'Who said we think it's funny?' Chris' voice was sharp. 'You think we like people backing off when we say who we are? We've had the lies and crap about us for years now. Cathy will have to get used to it.'

Dev said, wearily, 'Leave it Chris. The Legend is here. Can't you see it's grabbed Julie already?'

She was angry, like a small bristling cat. 'You're not going to pretend you are misunderstood choir boys? It's not Cathy's fault, all this trouble. It's all *your* fault, Dev. You got her pregnant. You made the scandal. Got into the punch-up with the police. You called the press and gave the interview to the papers and stirred up all the fans so we couldn't move outside the flat here. And then there was all the trouble at the College with the fans and the students and the police. You're the one to blame and *she's* getting expelled.'

'Julie,' Nick said, 'You can't talk to Dev like that.'

Dev ignored him, his eyes unreadable. 'That's life, sweetie. Tough. The wicked always win.'

She was nearly crying. 'It's her whole life. All she thinks of. Just painting. *What's she going to do?*'

'She'll be married to me,' said Dev and laughed, without humour. 'Happy Ever After, like the paper says.'

Julie did not hear the bitter note in his voice. 'You're *pleased*, aren't you? That she's out of the College. I suppose it's the reason she's going to marry you after all. She's been saying she wouldn't long enough. I suppose you knew it would be the last straw for her. How did you manage it?'

There was a brief silence, and then Chris said, tightly, 'Listen, Julie, listen good. Dev was on the phone all day yesterday and most of the evening trying to get a reversal of the College's decision. He got the Director. He's on our side, but it's a Governors' decision. So Dev talked to each and every one of them. They won't change their minds because they need a scapegoat for their mishandling of the situation when the student rioting started. They need someone to take the blame, for the damage to the building, for the fighting with the police. And they're frightened of more student troubles. All Dev got was a load of shit thrown at him. Cathy's *out* – permanently.'

Julie drew in a deep breath. She looked at Dev. 'Okay.'

He shrugged and smiled. 'That's life, sweetie.'

Chapter Two

When Julie got back to the flat in the late afternoon, Chris had gone but Dev was still there. He had changed into jeans and a sweatshirt and was sitting cross-legged and barefoot, on the bathroom floor, surrounded by slips of paper covered with private code marks in his large spiky writing, an empty six-pack of Carlsberg Special and a multi-track portable recorder which looked as though it had cost the earth. A guitar was propped against the bath and he was listening, totally absorbed, to the tape, which played the same explosion of sound over and over again, indistinguishable to Julie's ears, but not, apparently, to Dev, who made a disgusted sound, swore, and turned the machine off.

'It sounded all right to me,' Julie said, 'What's it called?'

Dev grunted. *'Message from Anarres.* Our new album. Cathy's idea. She's been reading Ursula le Guin.'

Julie, used to eccentricity, said curiously, 'Do you always use the bathroom floor?'

Dev raised an eyebrow, his eyes gleaming. 'For *music!*' Julie said, hastily.

'This bathroom's got a really nice live sound. You could hire it out. There's a spooky double echo in the higher registers. Hear?' He played a few chords on his guitar.

'No,' said Julie.

'Christ, you must be stone deaf,' he said exasperated. 'You wanting to use the john?'

'No,' said Julie, annoyed at being thrown out of her own bathroom. 'Where's Cathy?'

'Lying down. Shut the door after you.'

But instead, Julie found Cathy standing in the lounge looking out of the window into the darkening area. The room was bitterly cold, but Cathy seemed unaware of it.

'Dev's taken over the bathroom,' Julie said, throwing down her holdall and lighting the gas fire. 'Honestly, musicians are really crazy and screwed up. Not like art students.'

Cathy turned and smiled. 'Or fashion students. You're back early. Did the man from Fun Girl Modes see your rainbow disco dresses?'

'He took away my folder of designs but I don't suppose I'll hear until after Christmas.' She unwound her woolly scarf and threw her raincoat over the back of a chair. 'It seems funny without the fans outside.'

'The press were here again. But Dev talked to them and they went away. No problem.'

Julie watched her uneasily. 'You don't look well, Cathy. Is everything all right?'

'Dev's fixed the wedding. The day after tomorrow. St. Michael's Nethercombe. Four o'clock. You're all invited.'

'Oh great! I'm so glad. I'm sure you're doing the right thing.'

Cathy smiled mockingly. 'Marrying a millionaire? Gold taps in every bathroom...?'

'Cathy!'

'Sorry. Well, I'm glad it's settled. No more hassles, no more deciding, no more worries.'

'But, I mean, you are *happy* about it, aren't you?'

'Don't try to turn it into the romance of the century, Julie. You know I have to marry him. I couldn't earn enough to keep myself and bring the baby up. I couldn't even go out to work with a tiny baby to look after. I've nowhere to live and nothing to live on. Julie, that's one thing I've learned from this business. I'm never, ever, going to get into that trap again. Somehow I'm going to find a way to get some money of my own. Be independent.'

'But Cathy, you do like Dev a lot, whatever you say.' Julie coloured. 'I mean, you are having his baby. And when you're together anyone can see the electricity sizzling.'

Cathy said, strained, 'Maybe. But you don't understand, Julie. There are a lot of things between me and Dev you don't know about. It started very badly. He...he...' But the words would not come. The muscles in her throat had tightened into their familiar neurotic paralysis. She coughed and swallowed convulsively.

Julie stared at her pale face, mystified. 'But surely it can't be all that bad. Dev wouldn't do anything to hurt you. He's crazy about you. He's a nice guy.'

Cathy turned back to the window. There was a dusty potted geranium on the window sill and she rubbed a leaf between her thumb and finger absently. 'You'd be surprised what a nice guy can do sometimes, Julie. It's not just men in raincoats in dark alleys, you know.'

There was a long, shocked silence as Julie took in the implications of what she had said.

'You don't mean...You're not trying to tell me that *Dev*...'

'Did you know that more than half of the rapes in this country are committed by people known to the victims? Friends of the family, relatives, friends of the husband, business associates, husbands. I expect nearly all of them are usually nice guys too.'

Julie said, angrily, '*Husbands*? Are you crazy? It sounds like something you read in *Spare Rib*. I just don't believe this. You ought to be careful what you're saying, Cathy. People might take it the wrong way.'

'Chris is a nice guy too. He knew what Dev was going to do. He didn't stop him.'

Julie stared at her. 'Look, Cathy, I know you've been under a tremendous amount of strain these last few weeks, but you've got to stop making these wild accusations. There must have been some misunderstanding. You just wouldn't be able to stay in the same room with him if he'd – well, done what you said. And yet you're going to marry him. Have his baby. And don't tell me you don't want Dev. I've seen the way you are when he kisses you.'

'I don't understand how I can go on seeing him either, Julie. But those other women – they go on too. Living with it. Living with their husbands. What else can you do? Maybe they love them enough to forgive them.'

'You've forgiven Dev?'

Cathy stared at her, silent. Her fingers tightened and the geranium leaf broke off.

'You're making a mess on the carpet,' Julie pointed out.

'Sorry.' She picked up the pieces of leaf she had torn apart. 'Julie, let's forget we ever had this conversation, shall we?'

'I certainly don't want to remember it,' said Julie, indignantly.

'Let's change the subject then. Julie, tell me if my black skirt and chiffon top will be okay for the wedding.'

Julie said, horrified, 'But there will be hundreds of people there and the television and the photographers...'

'I can't go shopping! I'll be recognised and they'll follow me about and push and spit at me again...' Cathy's voice rose.

Julie could have kicked herself. She realised suddenly that Cathy must be very near breakdown. Although she had appeared to be calm and determined, it must have been a horrible experience to have to struggle through crowds of hostile fans, to have the most intimate details of her life spread out all over the world's newspapers. The worry, the pressure to marry Dev, the difficulty of deciding what to do about the baby and now being stopped from doing the only thing she really wanted to do...Julie thought it was going to take her a very long time to recover.

'I was going to offer my Degree gown, Cathy. It's your size. In fact I was going to ask you to model it in the dress show at the end of the year.'

'But you've worked so hard on it. It's the most important thing in your collection. I might spill something on it, or the fans might tear it...'

Julie laughed. She said, bluntly, 'Cathy if you can tell some of those newspaper people I designed the dress, I won't even *need* a degree. The publicity alone will start me in business.'

Cathy flushed, embarrassed.

'Come and try it on.' Julie grabbed her hand, excited. 'I brought it back from the College specially.'

The dress fitted perfectly. Julie had found the fabric in Paris in the summer. It was a delicate floating gauze, woven with gold threads. She had used wide bands of gold lace around the neck and around the full sleeves and hem. It was beautiful and unusual, and Cathy stared at herself in the mirror incredulously.

'You'll need something for your hair,' Julie said. 'Flowers, I think. I've got some of this fabric left. I could make some flowers with seed pearl centres to wear by your ears holding your hair back, like the maidens in those Victorian paintings.'

'Maiden?' Cathy arched her back and stuck her stomach out, laughing.

'Oh Cathy, you know you're so slim nobody will notice.'

Cathy looked again into the mirror at the golden reflection. She had recognised it instantly. The faery figure from a recurring childhood dream. The same gold hair, the silk gold dress, but always in the dream the figure had been smiling and serene, carrying trailing sprays of honeysuckle.

'...sandals and flowers,' Julie was saying. 'You'll have to get your brother to give you away. Has Dev got the ring?'

14

'Ring?' Cathy tensed suddenly. *With this ring...Wilt thou have this Man to thy wedded husband...obey and serve him, love, honour and keep him...for richer for poorer, in sickness and in health, to love, cherish...obey...till death...*

She slid out of the wedding dress quickly, pulled on her jeans and sweater and ran frantically along the hall.

'Dev,' she said, desperately. 'I *can't!* Why did you arrange a church ceremony? I can't swear all those things. I don't believe in religion.'

He got up. 'It shouldn't bother you then.' His voice was flippant, but his eyes were hard and glittering.

'We could get married in a Registry Office...'

'What you mean is you feel a Registry Office wedding is somehow not so serious. Easier to walk away from, without too much trouble.'

'No!'

'That's why we're getting married in a church. I'm tying you up as tight as I know how, Cathy. There's no get out now.'

'I won't promise to obey and serve!'

He smiled suddenly. 'All right, we'll tell the Vicar to leave that out. But the other's hold, Cathy. Love, cherish. Till death.' He put his arms around Cathy and held her close against him. He put his long fingers under her chin and turned her face up to him. 'I'll look after you now, Cathy.' He slid his mouth over hers, slowly, the pressure increasing, forcing her lips to open.

Julie, who had followed her, worried, looked away, and did not see Cathy shaking, a gleam of perspiration at her hairline.

There was so much to do the time passed swiftly. Cathy did what she was told, ate when something was put in front of her, made suggestions and telephone calls, but everything seemed unreal. She could not believe she would soon be married.

Dev and Chris, and Julie too, now, remained on guard and two days later she was married to Dev in Nethercombe Parish Church amid scenes of riot and confusion not seen in the village since Cromwell's men had marched in, three hundred years before.

Inside the church, the small handful of family and friends were outnumbered by famous pop faces, by newsmen from all over the world, by photographers, and television teams. The noise of the excited fans and sightseers who had made their way to the village to catch a glimpse of the celebrities, the ice cream and hot-dog vans, angry villagers and irritable policemen, trying to hold back the surging crowds, halted the ceremony twice, which could scarcely be heard above the din outside. Afterwards Cathy found she could remember only a few things from that time, but they were brilliantly clear and focussed like a surrealist painting.

There was her room, cleaned and empty, on the day of the wedding. All her gear and paintings had been taken down to Cox's Farm, Dev's house in the country, by one of the Easy Connection road vans, and there was nothing left. It was as though only a ghost girl had painted there and now she was gone forever.

'Is anything the matter, Cathy?'

She spun round and smiled brilliantly at Alun and Julie standing in the open doorway. 'Everything's fine.'

'You've been crying,' said Julie, angrily. 'What are you doing here? I left you bathing and brushing your hair.'

'Wedding nerves. I'm all right.' Cathy laughed. She came over and put her arm around Julie's waist. 'Thanks for everything, Julie, Alun. Tell the others?'

Julie was to be Maid of Honour. She looked
sophisticated in a deep blue lace suit, her hair put up so she
could wear a wide brimmed hat with a rose. She nodded.

'Be careful,' said Alun, 'the raw edges are showing.'

Outside the church, amid the shrieking and pushing
crowd, a familiar face came into focus like an omen. An
Easy Connection fan. The boy who had been outside the
College when she had been at her lowest ebb, realising she
would have to marry Dev.

'You don't have to stay for ever,' he had said.

'Let him in,' she said to one of the policemen holding
back the crowd.

'There's no room, Miss,' he said, smiling.

'He can stand at the back.'

Then she was in the church, crowded with faces she
recognised but did not know. Dev had been busy inviting
his friends. She saw Keith Hurst, Easy Connection's
drummer and his wife Lisa, smiling at her and waving.
Gratefully she tried to smile back.

Jim, her brother, was giving her away. He took her arm,
looking uncomfortable in his best suit. Their quarrel had
been patched up after a fashion. But it was his fault she was
here today, she thought bitterly.

Someone thrust a small bouquet of tiny white roses and
trailing honeysuckle into her hands. The scent made her
feel sick, reminding her of that terrible first night in the
apple orchard at Cox's Farm. She looked at the door
desperately, but Julie moved quickly into place behind her
and the organ began to play.

Dev's eyes were darker and more intense than she had
ever seen them. She heard her own voice, soft, husky,
promising impossible things to God. She tried to look away
from Dev's eyes, but they held hers fiercely and she was
promising him too. Then Dev, his voice shaking, his fingers

crushing hers, 'With this ring I thee wed, with my body I thee worship...'

At last it was over. They were in the vestry, signing their names and everybody was kissing everybody else. There were Dev's father and mother. Grey, middle aged, with glasses. Incredible they should have produced brilliant, rebellious Dev. Why had he never mentioned them or taken her to see them? She kissed his mother, who was crying and hugging her and saying over and over again, 'I'm so glad. I'm so *glad!'*

And suddenly, there was Chris Carter. Ashen. Not smiling. His back turned to the crowd. 'The Best Man gets to kiss the Bride, too, Cathy.'

It was not a Best Man's kiss. It was a lover's kiss, and her body reacted with the same sexual fire as it did when Dev touched her. She struggled away from him, horrified. He smiled slowly, his eyes shining, challenging.

Chapter Three

Most of the guests and all the media came back to Cox's Farm. There were too many people. Perspiring waiters thrust through the crowds. The caterers worked desperately to refill the plates of canapés and smoked salmon.

Now it was all over, the action taken, Cathy felt lightheaded, manic with the release of tension. She stood laughing and talking with the famous faces she had only ever seen on the television or in the newspapers, Dev's arm clamped round her tightly as though she would run away if he let her go. She drank the wine and drove the silver knife deep into the towering wedding cake, Dev's hand bearing down on hers. They all cheered, and were very kind to her. The legends about the generosity of show biz people were all true, Cathy thought.

As it got later and the more respectable guests and the media went, the party got progressively wilder. The music seared the ears with sound, the champagne flowed too freely and more than one of the famous faces were stoned on something other than drink. She watched some of the guests outside throwing others into the floodlit, heated, swimming pool and hoped they could swim. It had turned into the sort of wild rock party she had heard about.

'That is the secret of life, young Cathy,' said Tom Gibbon, tall and lean, behind her, breathing drunkenly into her ear.

She laughed at him. 'Throw other people into the swimming pool first?'

He stared into her eyes solemnly. 'Learn it fast and learn it young and don't forget it: This is the ballroom of the Titanic.'

'Right,' said Chris, putting his arm around Tom's shoulders and swaying with him. 'Remember good ol' Jim Morrison.'

Tom and Chris shouted together loudly, 'NO ONE HERE GETS OUT ALIVE!'

For a moment Cathy felt an icy warning spiral up her spine, then Tom swept her into a frenzied dance routine, which had nothing to do with the music being played. He was a superb dancer.

Cathy felt wild and reckless. She laughed and danced, and danced, closing her mind to her anxiety and doubts, determined to enjoy herself. Tom Gibbon was right – just live for the present and enjoy it.

She changed from the beautiful gold dress, afraid it would get spoiled, to her black skirt and sea-green, see-through top, and stood for a while in the entrance hall with Dev. He was talking to people who were leaving. She couldn't hear what they were saying through the crashing, amplified rock, but she smiled and nodded like a wind-up doll.

Across the hall she saw Chris arguing with Julie. Julie was shaking her head fiercely, but when he put his arm around her and whispered in her ear, she leaned her head against his shoulder helplessly and went upstairs with him.

At the bend, where the staircase turned, Chris looked back, as though feeling Cathy's gaze on him. He smiled at her mockingly and went on up.

Cathy was furious and something deep inside was hurting very much more than it ought. Her exhilaration drained away, and suddenly she was conscious of her bone tiredness. She thought that if she didn't sit down soon she would collapse.

Dev turned to her, laughing. For a moment they were alone in the entrance. 'I don't know how he does it.'

She realised he too had been watching Chris and Julie. 'Very clever.'

'You're jealous, Cathy.'

'No I'm *not*. I'm not jealous. I don't like him using my friend, that's all. She was engaged and happy before he came, and now she's in love with him and he doesn't care. It's not fair.'

'He can't have what he wants so he takes the next best thing. Somebody near you.'

'Dev...'

'It's no good pretending, Cathy. I saw him kiss you in the vestry. Besides, he's never made any secret of it.'

'Do you tell each other everything?' Her voice was sour.

'Pretty well. We've been together so long, we know anyway. Now you're jealous again. Of me, this time.' She flushed. 'How do you feel about *him*, Cathy? How did you feel when he kissed you?'

She refused to look at him, and he turned up her face, reading the answer. He exhaled slowly. 'Just don't let him kiss you too often, that's all. Do you hear me? You're my wife now. He's not going to get you.'

He put his arms around her and held her gently against him.

'You looked so beautiful today, Cathy. I never saw anything so lovely. I want you so much.'

He kissed her until he felt her trembling. She tried to put her arms around his neck, but he saw her skin was a queer greenish white and damp with perspiration. He let her go at once and stood away.

'Dev – I'm sorry.'

His voice hardened. 'All right. I said if you married me I'd wait for the loving. Nothing's changed.'

'I'm sorry,' she said again, formally.

He spun round. 'I need a drink. Where is everyone?'

It seemed as though the party would go on forever. Exhausted, Cathy found a refuge in the kitchen with Mrs. Kaye, the housekeeper and cook. She was a placid, quiet woman, apparently undisturbed by the party raging outside. Cathy was not to worry, she said, the mess would be cleared up very quickly next day with extra help from the village. She talked about her grown-up children and Christmas presents and when she went off duty at two o'clock, back to her cottage next to the entrance gates in the drive, Cathy felt more human than she had felt all day. She stayed in the kitchen, curled up in a Windsor chair by the Aga, half-hidden by an oak dresser and dozed off in the warmth and quiet.

She was awakened by the sound of one of the guests moving around, making tea. Dark, glossy hair, dark eyes, dramatic craggy face. She groped in the recesses of her mind and came up with his name. Dave Hampton. One of the inner circle of Dev's friends, a superb guitarist with a band called Night Mission. She remembered that he had tried to help her once.

'Hello, Dave.'

'Cathy.' He turned, smiling at her. 'What are you doing here?'

'Sleeping.' She stretched and yawned and came to the table. 'You're not drunk like the others.'

'I get sick, not drunk.' He grinned.

'So do I,' she said, and laughed bleakly at her own private joke.

He looked at her, curious. 'This is a funny place to spend your wedding night.'

'Is there a cup for me too?'

'You don't mind, do you? I've got to drive back to Earl's Court soon. We've got a gig in Glasgow tomorrow night. I mean tonight now.'

'I don't mind. It's not my kit...' She stopped dead and went red.

He laughed. 'You'll get used to it.'

They sat drinking the tea companionably.

'Dev said you'd painted a picture of that gig we did together at Azra's. I'd really like to see it.'

'You mean, *now*?'

'If you've nothing else to do.'

She laughed. 'No, I've nothing else to do. Come on then, I think they put my paintings in Dev's studio.'

The entrance was deserted now, and the sounds of revelry concentrated around the garden room and the pool. They went up the wide, scarlet-carpeted stair, and Cathy looked uncertainly along the corridor of heavy doors. 'I'm not sure where it is. I've only been here once before.' She switched her mind away, refusing to remember what had happened to her then, and began opening doors quickly.

They found the paintings easily enough, in a big empty room at the end of the corridor, with windows facing north. They were propped against the walls. She turned them for Dave to see and walked away, not wanting to look at them herself.

Dev's few canvases were on the other side of the room, probably dating from the time he had been a student at the London College of Art before he had become a professional musician. She looked through them curiously.

They were abstract paintings, showing a strange, original vision. Nothing in them was substantial. They were all in a state of flux, and it was impossible to identify the shapes. Diamonds, fire, light, always it was changing, slipping, escaping from a shape like a stretched-out hand. She stared at the paintings, trying to understand. Was this his experience of life - things forever sliding away as he grasped them, everything dissolving so quickly that nothing remained permanent? His life as a touring musician must have made that feeling worse. Was that why he had grabbed at her so fiercely, why he could not risk her getting away?

She wanted to go to him and ask, but the idea seemed ridiculously impossible. The last time she had seen him, some hours ago, he was having a drinking contest with Tom Gibbon and another young man, Leo Field, Easy Connection's bassist. They were yelling with laughter, surrounded by a shouting crowd, and the wine was running out of their mouths, down their chins and chests, staining their white wedding shirts like blood and dripping unheeded on the pale carpet. Not a good time to choose. He must be very drunk now and she had no illusions. Dev, drunk, was very dangerous indeed.

Behind her, she heard Dave speaking. 'I'm sorry?'

'I said, I had no idea you were so good. This painting – it's brilliant. How did you know I feel like that when I play? It's me and my music as well. And Azra's. How I felt in that special place on that special night, playing that special music. You've got it all.' He sounded rueful, shaken. 'You've blown my cover.'

Cathy flushed with pleasure. 'I'm trying to paint people, how they think and feel, in their places.'

He hesitated. 'I want to ask a question, but it sounds bigheaded. I mean, why *me*? Where's Dev? He was there that night.'

'We had a row about that. It was just that I had sketches of you. I was drawing you all through the set before Dev arrived. I've been drawing musicians for months. You can stare at them, you see, and it doesn't matter. I do Zen drawing. Relaxation and meditation. But that night, it was special.'

'This painting, is it for sale?'

'It's sold. Caleb Crow of the Arundell Gallery owns it. He just hasn't collected it yet.'

He turned another painting. 'Is this one sold too?'

'Yes, I'm contracted.'

'You were with this guy at Azra's.' He looked at her sideways. She forced herself to look at the painting. Nick, lying on the sofa in Hamilton Square on a quiet Sunday afternoon, his body brown and loose. Nick had said he couldn't come to the wedding and she was grateful. If she had married Nick – if he had asked her – where would she be now? In a small country hotel, probably, somewhere quiet to suit both of them, lying in his arms warm and *safe*.

Suddenly she found she was nearly crying. What was she doing here, wandering in a fog of unreality in a big rich house, full of drunken strangers?

She turned her head away, but not before he had seen.

'I said something wrong?'

'No. It'll work itself out. It's got to.'

He looked at her for a few moments longer and saw she really did not want to talk about it.

'What are you working on now?'

She shook her head, her eyes frightened. 'It'll be hard, working here. The atmosphere...I'd forgotten it was so...imprisoning.'

He looked at her with concern. 'It'll be better when we all go. A rock musician's life – it's kind of strange. But you'll get used to it. We all do. Well, most of us. You're too good to stop painting. That crazy artist friend of Dev's, Tom Gibbon, was toasting you as the best thing since Hockney.'

'He said that?' She smiled, her sense of humour reviving. 'He must be as drunk as Dev.'

He grinned at her. 'Drunker. Can you imagine that bunch at art college together – Dev, Chris, *and* Tom?'

She laughed aloud. He took her hand and smiled at her. 'I hope you'll be happy, Cathy. Dev is a hard case, but there's a lot there when you get through the fortifications. And I'll bet you will work here. Because you have to, don't you? It's an obsession.'

She stared at him. 'Now you've blown *my* cover.'

'I read the tea leaves as well.'

They laughed, relaxing the tension, and went downstairs, holding hands lightly, and she felt better.

Dev was nowhere to be seen, but Chris, lounging on the leather sofas in the entrance hall, with a tall glass of colourless liquid in his hand, watched them narrowly, his eyes hostile.

'Where have you been, Cathy? Looking at the etchings?'

Dave raised an eyebrow. Cathy said, keeping her voice carefully controlled, 'I don't think it's anything to do with you, Chris.'

'Dev's my friend.'

'Meaning?' Dave's voice was edgy.

'You can leave our little baby alone. I thought you had your hands full with Janey Adams. Or has Jay Bird got his leg over permanently?'

Dave went white, and Cathy was aware of his hurt. He would be no match for Chris, vicious at in-fighting.

Dave said, with an effort, '*Dev's* baby, surely?'

Chris' face changed and he swayed to his feet dangerously.

Cathy said, bitingly, 'You're drunk, Chris. Don't try to pick a fight. I was showing Dave my painting of Azra's. And now he's driving back to town and I'm going to see him out, especially as your good friend Dev seems not to be around. Perhaps you'd better go back to bed and sleep it off.'

She turned her back on him and went with Dave to the big front door. 'I'm sorry. Chris is good at going for the jugular, isn't he? I didn't know you were with Janey Adams. She's my favourite female singer.'

'I thought everyone knew about us.' He smiled lopsidedly. 'She had a concert in Brussels or she'd have been here. We've been together a while, but it's rocky. Both of us in the music business. She's always working and I've got this Australian tour coming up...'

Cathy remembered Janey Adams on her television show, dark and intense, her voice honey gold, her long expressive hands, sweeping heavy hair. 'She's beautiful. I'd love to paint her one day.'

'I'll tell her.'

'I hope it works out for you, Dave.'

He took her hand, but on impulse, bent and kissed her lightly.

'You too, Cathy.'

She shut the door and made her way back to the kitchen, ignoring Chris, stretched out on the sofa, watching her. As she passed he said softly, menacing, 'Keep away from Dave Hampton.'

She stopped, half-laughing. 'Or you'll do what?'

'I'll stop him.' His voice was quiet, expressionless, but Cathy was cold, suddenly aware of the tamped down violence in him. She remembered him hitting the policeman in Hamilton Square. How had she ever imagined that Chris was easy-going and relaxed?

'Mind your own business, Chris.'

'You are my business, Cathy. Everything you do. Everything you think. Everything you feel. *My* business. And I'm *your* business. Me and Dev and you.'

'You're crazy.'

He smiled, cat and mouse. 'You'll see.'

At first light she found a thick jacket and walked out of the house across the lawn and fields down to the stream running through the water meadow. She sat on a large stone and watched the sun come up. The early morning light was brilliant, glittering on the frosted grass.

She could see the strange tree trunk she had painted months ago when it had all started. But everything else had changed. The green had gone and the tangled undergrowth was a pattern of black interlocking lines with filigree edges.

Dev and Chris had stepped out of the trees like woodland spirits and stared at her. They were fair and beautiful in the evening sunlight, like the Elven Lords of an ancient ballad. And like the old ballads, they had been full of destruction and violence. She shivered.

She must try to put the past, what had happened, behind her. She must try to live each day as it came. No one here gets out alive. She must break this nightmare of unreality, this deathly dream state that kept spreading over her.

She looked up and Chris was there again, standing watching her, hunched. But he looked wild, dishevelled, unshaven, and there was a line of tiredness or pain between his eyes. She felt there was no kindness in him, only pain and malice.

'Dev's out cold, you'll have to wait. He must be mad.'

She turned her head away. So Dev had not told him about their bargain. Her heart lightened. She said, dryly, patting her stomach, 'The marriage has been consummated already, Chris.'

She saw his face then, and was sorry. She got up and walked to the stream, her back to him.

'Why did you kiss me like that in the church?'

'I felt like it.'

'Dev saw you.'

He shrugged. 'So what? He knows I want you. He knows everything I think.'

'Chris, please don't be like this. Julie saw too. I thought we were friends.'

'I don't like being on my own. I'm shut out.'

'You'll see Dev more than I will. Recording. Touring. You only want me because Dev wants me. You have plenty of girls.'

'You don't understand even now, do you, Cathy? Don't want to understand.'

Cathy's voice shook. 'Don't start talking about Karma again. You're just trying to make trouble. You never said anything to me before. Never kissed me even.'

'That day, when you found out we were Easy Connection, the door slammed shut. I saw it. You wouldn't have loved me or married me. But Dev was clever, or more desperate maybe. And his timing was bloody lucky. He got you pregnant. And now I've only got to hang around and wait.'

'What are you saying?' she whispered, horrified.

'I'm warning you. Don't think of me as a friend, Cathy. You're not going to live happy ever after with Dev. Think of me as a vulture. I'm away up there, circling around. And I'm waiting. Watching and waiting.'

Chapter Four

After the wedding the chaos was cleared away as if by magic. A famous firm came and replaced the pale green carpet in the garden room, ruined with red wine and ground-out cigarettes. The swimming pool was drained so that various articles of clothing, two chairs and a smashed television could be removed, and Leo Field's brand new butter-yellow Alfa Romeo was towed out of the old duck pond, where he had been trying to prove it would float. It had been a good party.

Everything was serene and orderly again, and Cathy did not see the three security men walking the park, and turning back fans and sightseers at the gates.

Dev and Chris were out most of the day, working long hours in the recording studio in town and returning very late, long after Cathy had gone to bed.

'I'm sorry we're out so much just now, Cathy,' Dev said. 'But we have to get this album done by the end of February. It's a double album. Our best ever. Better than *Head Start* even.'

'Why February?'

'Because we start the tour to Japan and Australia then.'

'You mean you'll be away?'

Dev looked at her sharply. 'I told you. For three months.'

'I'm sorry, I forgot.' She tried to keep the elation from her voice. Free again. For a while.

'We're coming home via the States, but we only have a couple of concerts there this time. I'll do the album mix when I get back, and it will be ready for release in September before our big tour of the States.'

'How long will that be?'

'Another three months.' Dev took her hand. 'I'm really sorry, Cathy. It was all arranged before I ever met you. We work years ahead. We can't cancel. Do you mind?'

'Of course not,' Cathy said, surprised. 'It's your work. Why should you cancel?'

'Because you're going to have a baby, remember? You ought not to be left alone. I ought to be with you. But Mrs. Kaye and George and the security men will be here. Dr. Eliot in the village is coming up, and I've hired a Harley Street man, as well as...'

Cathy said, politely, 'Well, it's nice of you to go to all that trouble, Dev, but I'm not a porcelain doll. There's no need to set all these minders on to me. I'm used to looking after myself.'

Dev laughed derisively. 'You haven't made much of a job of it so far.'

'I got a place in a famous college, found a place to live, got a grant...'

'And got expelled.'

'That's not fair. You know it wasn't my fault.' Cathy was angry. 'I was doing all right until I met you. Why are you trying to put me down?'

Dev ruffled her hair, amused. 'Of course, you'll be coming with us to the States in September.'

'Three months?' Cathy said, dismayed. 'But Dev, what about *my* work?'

He shrugged. 'Maybe you can do some sketching. I want you with me, Cathy. You don't have to make money and the painting can wait. Besides, you're not working yet, are you?'

Cathy drew a difficult breath. 'No, not yet.'

She had set up her easel in Dev's studio, unpacked her paints and stretched two new canvases. She had looked through her portfolio at the drawings and studies, ideas for paintings, waiting for that deep slow curl of excitement which always heralded the start of a new painting. But nothing happened. She felt blank and empty, and the sketches were meaningless, like the work of a stranger.

She pulled on her jacket and walked out into the dank winter countryside, trying not to panic. Give it time, she thought. It would come back. When she felt calmer and more settled. When she got back into her skull. When she broke the invisible barrier, it would come back. Hadn't she always known it would be difficult to work in that house? The thick carpets, the expensive furniture and original paintings, it was like trying to live on a film set or in a museum. She had the huge pink bedroom across from Dev's. It had rosewood furniture, French handprinted wallpaper alive with flowers and birds, and its own bathroom, with a round marble bath sunken into deep pile rose carpet. It made her feel uneasy and guilty. The cost of the bath alone would keep a poor Indian family in food for a couple of years, she thought. She wandered about the house restlessly, unable to settle, still wound up from the stress of the past weeks. She had no idea what she was expected to do.

Mrs. Kaye ran the house and cooked. Her husband George looked after the cars and the garden, with the help of a boy from the village. Two women came in daily and had finished cleaning before Cathy was awake.

For the first time in her life there was nothing Cathy had to do, nowhere she had to go. No school. No college. No lectures. No studying. No shopping for food or cooking. No cleaning or laundry. No need to get up early. No need to get up at all really.

She said, at last, 'Is there anything you think I ought to be doing here, Dev?'

He grinned. 'Polish the parquet? Scrub the kitchen?'

Cathy smiled back. 'I know it sounds stupid, but well, I just can't see how to fit in. Mrs. Kaye says she doesn't want any help in the kitchen...'

'You don't have to do anything, Cathy. Just enjoy yourself.' He grinned again. 'You can play all our CDs and watch the videos.'

'I can't,' said Cathy, laughing. 'I'm scared of turning that thing on. I'm scared of touching *anything* in case I break it or make a mess.'

'For chrissakes, Cathy, it's just a pad to live in!'

Cathy said, flushed and embarrassed, 'But I want to do my job. I mean I ought...well, I'd *like* to try to make things as comfortable as possible for you. That's what good wives do, don't they? Arrange things as you want. See you get the food you like. My mother always said...'

Dev laughed. 'What do golden-haired lovelies like you know about running a house?'

Cathy said, annoyed, 'A lot. Where I come from all the girls know how to cook and clean. Their mothers have to go out to work. Looks have nothing to do with it.'

'Leave it to Mrs. Kaye, that's what she's paid for.' He got up and put his hands on her shoulders. 'I don't want a hausfrau, Cathy. I want a wife.' He kissed her softly. 'And a lover.'

Boredom drove her along the lane to see her sister-in-law, Mary, at the Police House, but they were stiff and uncomfortable together. Mary could only talk about Dev's cars and the furnishings of the Farm, and Cathy found that deep down she was still blaming Mary for putting pressure on her to marry Dev. A little help from Mary and Jim and she could have remained free and brought the baby up herself. When Mary started on about the coming baby, she made an excuse and left.

She didn't want to talk about the baby with anyone. Her feelings about it were so chaotic and changeable. Sometimes resentful and deeply angry, sometimes fearful, anxious, guilty, and increasingly, since she had got married and come to live at the Farm, she felt a rising excitement and anticipation. She knew she needed time to sort it all out in her mind. Mrs. Kaye said comfortably that it was changes in her hormone levels, which were responsible for her mood swings, but Cathy knew it went deeper and was to do with what had happened between Dev and herself, and perhaps, even, to do with her own father, who had walked out on them one day and never come back.

On Christmas Eve even Chris went away, groaning and reluctant, to his parents for the holiday.

'Is he going to live here all the time?' Cathy asked Dev.

'Sure, why not? It's big enough.'

'Hasn't he got a place of his own?'

'A flat next to mine near Sloane Square. But it's better for him to be here. More convenient for writing songs. You know he mostly does the lyrics. Besides we like each other around.' He looked at her narrowly. 'Why shouldn't he live here?'

Cathy shrugged, feeling uneasy. Since he had kissed her she was too aware of Chris, the muscular litheness of his body, his light-grey eyes watching her.

'What's his father like?'

Dev grinned. 'You'll be shocked. Red in tooth and claw. A genuine capitalist. He's a stockbroker. Even lives in Surrey.'

'Your father isn't exactly a revolutionary – Chief Accountant of Imperial Petroleum.'

Dev made a rude noise.

'Couldn't we go to see your parents?' Cathy said, wistfully. 'I've not met them properly, and well, it would be nice to be part of a family again. I miss my mother.'

'We are a family.' Dev's smile had disappeared. 'I don't get on with my old man, Cathy. We don't see each other more than's necessary.'

'But your mother was so nice at the wedding.'

'Yeah. Too *nice*. She's a doormat and he walks all over her. We'll stay here for Christmas. On our own. Very romantic.'

Christmas was spent very quietly dozing on the sofa, with Dev's arms around her, watching the television. Although she had explained to him carefully her feelings about killing animals for fur coats, Dev had insisted upon buying her a fur coat for Christmas.

'You look terrific,' Dev said. 'You need some sexy dresses to go with it.'

'I won't wear them. I've got enough clothes anyway.'

'Jeans and sweaters. I'll buy you something more exciting.'

'I can buy my own clothes. I've still got some of my grant and the money Caleb gave me for the paintings.'

Dev laughed. 'You don't have to economise. I've opened a joint account. You can buy what you want.'

Cathy flushed. 'But it's not my money.'

'Ours.'

'I don't feel that.' Cathy took a breath. 'You don't understand, Dev. I want to be as independent as possible. I want to earn money for myself. I want...'

'I know what you want, sweetheart. I'm a better judge than you are.' He grinned at her wickedly and slid his hand across her stomach and caressed it gently.

Cathy pushed his hand away and stood up. She felt hot and confused.

'When I get back from this tour, Cathy, we'll have a special holiday. How do you feel about Tobago or Hawaii? I've never been to Hawaii.'

It sounded unlikely. Cathy laughed. 'Out of this world.'

'A real honeymoon, maybe?' Dev said softly, his eyes bright, questioning.

Cathy's colour deepened. 'There'll be the baby then.'

'That's okay. I've already fixed up a nursery nurse to look after him.'

Cathy said, slowly, disbelievingly, 'You engaged a nurse before I saw her?'

'It wasn't necessary for you to see her.'

Cathy was angry. 'But he's my baby. I want to see the woman who's going to look after him. How do I know she's the right person?'

'Good qualifications. A reference from the Earl of something. A Connection fan. *Nice.*' He grinned and described a voluptuous shape in the air with his hands. 'She'll be here in May.'

Cathy said furiously, 'Doesn't my opinion count at all?'

'That was one of your conditions wasn't it – when you said you'd marry me? Somebody to look after the baby and no sex.'

Cathy said, trying to hold on to her temper, 'I asked for a *motherly* person to help look after the baby in case I didn't feel right about him. And I asked you to promise not to bring your other women to the Farm while it was our home and the baby was here. The no-sex – that was *you*. You offered.'

Dev laughed. 'Yeah, that's right. I'd forgotten. I'll have to keep all those other women in town. I'll buy a hotel.' He laughed again and catching her hand, pulled her into his arms and kissed her. 'I love you crazy, Cathy. How can there be anyone else?'

'Not yet, maybe. I mean it Dev. Loyalty. Security. The place where I live. They're very important to me. My father...he left us and went off to Australia. I can't stand people who are disloyal. People who betray you. It's the worst crime.'

Dev was still laughing. 'Does that mean we can forget the no-sex. You've changed your mind?'

Cathy tried to move away. 'It means I'd like you to *listen* to me sometimes, Dev. Really hear what I say. It means I'd like to be asked before you take decisions about my baby. I know I'm young and I haven't had your experience, but there's no need for you to treat me like an incompetent kid. You're not my father, Dev.'

He was startled and angry. 'Are you sure you want to talk seriously, Cathy? If so there are things I'd like to talk about. Personal things, like what you feel about me. How I feel about you. About what happened that night we met.'

'No!' Cathy backed away.

Dev laughed. 'I thought not. Come on, give Daddy another kiss.'

Cathy kicked the door closed behind her and walked her anger and resentment off along the stream, wishing he did not arouse such intense physical feelings in her. Dev knew exactly how deeply her body reacted to his touch, and he had begun to take a malicious delight in seeing how far he could arouse her. He made no attempt to sleep with her, but on the other hand he hadn't promised not to touch or kiss her.

The worst thing about being married was the lack of privacy, Cathy sometimes thought. Dev walked freely in and out of her bedroom at any time he felt like it, and into her bathroom too, until she locked the door on him. He was very angry.

'Don't I get *any* privacy?' Cathy said, equally angry. 'You walk in when I'm taking a bath without knocking even. You watch me getting dressed. I'm – I'm not used to it.'

'I'm your husband, Cathy, in case you've forgotten. I've got rights if I choose to use them.'

Cathy's hands clenched, but she looked at him directly. 'Is that a threat? Are you saying you're going back on your promise after all?'

Dev groaned and pulled her against him. 'Cathy, I'm just saying I like to see you naked. That's not hurting you is it?' The colour flooded up into her face and burned darkly. He held her head gently between his hands, smoothing back her hair like a child and kissed her. 'Cathy, you've got to get used to me. To my hands, my mouth, my body. We're *married*. I promised not to have sex with you, but I won't be able to keep that promise for ever.'

He kissed her again, slowly, sensually, opening her mouth. Cathy put her arms round his body and allowed the waves of feeling to wash over her. She was trembling, clinging to him tightly, returning his kisses. His arms tightened around her suddenly, crushing her against him, his kisses getting heavier, out of control.

Cathy thrust him away, violently, and stood back gasping, her eyes shocked and frightened, her body taut, ready to run.

Dev closed his eyes and drew in a shuddering breath. 'Don't look like that,' he said, at last, huskily. 'I'm not going to rape you again. You won't believe this, Cathy, but I don't make a habit of it.'

'I'm sorry. It was just for the moment...'

'I did it *once,* when I was half-mad and drunk and desperate. You know I'd give anything now for it never to have happened. Anything to make it up to you. Can't you try to forgive me, Cathy?'

'Being sorry doesn't help, Dev. Apologising is no good.' Her eyes were full of tears. 'It's a feeling that comes over me. Sick fear. *Terror.* I can't do anything about it. Do you think I wouldn't, if I could? Do you think I'm a dummy? You touch me and kiss me and take me to the edge and then I can't do anything about it. The sickness comes. The fear. You're driving me mad, Dev.' Her voice rose.

'Cathy, that night – afterwards – you loved me then.'

She turned to the door quickly.

'Cathy, we've got to talk about it.'

'Just give me time. It'll be all right. I want to forget.'

'Cathy.'

She stopped, her back to him.

'It's all right. You're safe. But don't lock your door on me again, or I'll break it down.'

Chapter Five

Cathy was aware of a growing depression and edginess. At first she pretended to herself it was the hormone changes, or the sexual tension with Dev, but as the days passed she finally admitted to herself that it was because she had stopped painting.

She could not bring herself to pick up her brushes, even. The stranger she had become to herself had nothing to say. The paint and the brushes were useless.

All her life, in good times and in bad, painting had been her refuge. Always she had been able to shut off the outside world and its disasters by plunging deep into her work – when her father had left, when her mother had died – always there had been her work. Now she needed its comfort more than ever, but it had failed, leaving her lonelier and more vulnerable than ever before.

She was trapped behind the icy barrier she had erected to keep the pain and despair away, and she could not get in touch with her real feelings.

All the paintings she had planned seemed empty and meaningless. Even putting paint on to a canvas seemed stupid and a waste of time. Once or twice she tried to draw, but there was nothing to say, and her hands seemed clumsy and unable to perform. The great lift of the heart, the joyous anticipation that had always come when she thought of painting, seemed to have gone forever.

Caleb Crow telephoned, and she told him she was not working and that he had better cancel the contract. She thought he would be angry and say, 'I told you so,' but he only laughed.

'You're shell-shocked. You need time. You'll get over it, and I want you under contract to me. Get this bloody baby out of the way and you'll be all right. When did you say it's due?'

'May.'

'All right, now listen. I'm going to put some of your work in my Mixed Summer Show in June as starters. There's a lot of interest in the drawings and I want the critics to get a look at them before they disappear into private collections. If you've got any extra stuff, well and good. But in any case I'm reckoning on a major one-woman show in October. Got that? October.'

She almost laughed, and felt the bile bitter on her tongue. She swallowed and gritted her teeth. 'I told you. *I can't work.*'

'You crying?'

'No.' She rubbed away the tears.

'All right. We'll talk about it again later on.'

'*I tell you, it's no good!*' She shouted down the receiver, but already he had rung off.

In the New Year Chris came back, and suddenly the house was full of people and noise. Arrangements for the tour to Japan and Australia were fully under way.

Cars arrived at all times of the day and night, skidding on the gravelled drive. The telephone never stopped ringing and was answered by a young man with a thin serious face, Cal Bowman, who was Dev's personal assistant and roadie, or by bouncing Gregg Fisher, with waist-length hair, who was Chris' roadie.

Strange young men in jeans, dirty teeshirts and incredible hair styles camped in what had once been the billiard room, and began to overhaul Dev's collection of nearly ninety guitars, thirty of which would be going on tour with him. Men in suits arrived with briefcases and documents. The press arrived for a series of in-depth interviews for the music papers. Tuned-in ladies in arty clothes arrived to measure for stage clothes, and a building firm arrived with a bulldozer and concrete mixer and began to bash a hole through the side of the house and dig a three-metre wide driveway behind the apple orchard. They were building what Dev claimed would be the finest private recording studio in the UK when it was finished.

'But Dev, surely it could have waited a while, until you got back from Japan. All this noise and mess...'

'The building has to be done quickly. Then we can start to install the equipment before the US tour. We want to do our next album in our own studio. It's planned already. We're on a big creative high, Chris and me. We don't want to waste it.'

There was a glow of well-being about him. Energy and excitement seemed to pour out of him, even when he had had a long day and a long drive from town.

Cathy retreated to her bedroom. It seemed the only room in the house not full of strangers with curious, hostile eyes. The heavy banging and the all-pervading, highly amplified rock, made her feel physically ill.

After a while Dev found it convenient to use her room to prepare his production notes, ducking out of the madhouse below for an hour's peace. He said, grinning, that it was the only place in the house people wouldn't come knocking for him. After a while Chris came too, lying flat on the carpet, utterly relaxed, his eyes closed, his arms behind his head, arguing the lyrics with Dev, who sat cross-legged on her bed, propped against the bed head, his notes spread over the silken cover.

They looked beautiful, Cathy thought, their faces pure in concentration and creation, their bodies full of coiled energy and strength. She watched them with silent resentment. They had even taken over her bedroom now. They took over everything and everyone.

She went out, leaving them to it, and walked in the blustery wind, heavy with sleet, followed at a discreet distance by one of Dev's security men.

'I won't have it.' Cathy shouted, thumping the table with her fists.

'It's for your own protection, Cathy,' Dev said. 'There are all kinds of weirdos around. Kidnap threats.'

'No. I'm an ordinary person. It makes me feel like a prisoner. You have to listen to me this time Dev. I can't bear it.'

Dev sighed. 'Have it your way.'

Two days later she went into the local town to buy winter boots. George Kaye insisted on driving her, and the big car parked outside the store attracted attention. With incredible swiftness she was recognised, trapped in a corner and surrounded by a sea of avid faces and waving arms thrusting paper and pencils at her for autographs. It brought back all the horrors of the scenes outside the College and in Hamilton Square, where she had had to fight through groups of spitting, hostile Connection fans. At last the Manager came to her rescue and she was taken to the car, feeling sick and hysterical.

On the way home black depression clamped down, as she realised that Dev would hear all about it. She would never get away from the security men now.

At the Farm she found a group of roadies playing poker in the garden room, Bill Hopkins, Easy Connection's manager, and two more men shouting at each other in the dining room, and three workmen drinking tea with the Kayes in the kitchen. In her bedroom, Chris was lying on her bed reading a book.

'What's the matter, Cathy?'

She did not trust herself to speak. She went stonily into her bathroom and locked the door. She lay for a long time in a warm bath, shaking, looking at the pink marble and the plate-glass mirrors, feeling them closing in on her. Walls of mirror glass. Walls of people. Trapped. Imprisoned. She felt unable to breathe.

That evening she asked Dev if she could use the barn as a studio.

It was a strange building, away by itself at the other end of the swimming pool. Perhaps it had been a barn originally, or perhaps it was the original manor, because it was much older than the rest of the house. It was long and low with a stone floor and a wood-beamed roof. The wooden doors had been replaced at some point, with high glass windows, which looked away from the house across the empty meadows and parkland to woods and distant hills. When he bought the house Dev had intended to use it as the recording studio, but there was something wrong with the acoustics and the big space was still empty.

'A studio? I thought you weren't working.'

'Well, I'm not. Yet. I just thought...maybe if I had my own place...Somewhere I felt *free*...'

'What about the room upstairs. What's wrong with that?' Cathy could hear the gathering hostility in his voice.

'It's your studio. I'd like somewhere of my own. Away from the house. I feel in a prison...All these people...'

'It's too lonely out there. Not much heat.'

'I don't care. It's what I want.'

He stared at her through narrowed eyes. 'You trying to get away from me, Cathy?'

'I'd just like a quiet place. Where I can think. Be myself.'

He shrugged. 'It's your house. You can do what you want in it.'

She shook her head and tried to smile. 'Your house. I can't get used to it.'

Dev turned away. 'Do what you want, Cathy. But don't fool yourself – you are trying to escape. And it's me you're trying to escape from.'

She cleaned the big room herself, mopping the stone floor to a silvery sheen. In the attics of the house she found an old divan, a chair, a chest of drawers and a card table with a wobbly leg. There was an old carpet rolled up, which turned out to be Persian, intricate and glowing with subtle colour. George Kay and one of the workmen moved them all down for her.

She covered the divan with the red bedcover and the big cushions she had from Hamilton Square, set up her easel near the window and arranged her paints on the card table. A carpenter came and made a drying rack for her canvases and Cal Bowman rigged up spotlights to shine directly on her easel. Her sketches and drawings filled the chest of drawers and lay piled on the top, waiting.

For a while the activity had made her feel hopeful and happy, but when everything was ready she still did not start painting. Instead, she sat for hours on the divan, wrapped in her old duvet, watching the pale winter sunlight picking out the stark trees across the fields, or making the carpet glow on the worn stone.

'She's not eating hardly anything at all,' Mrs. Kaye told Dev, very worried. 'It's not natural for someone in her condition. The trays come back practically untouched.'

'You've got to eat, Cathy,' Dev said. He stood in the doorway of the barn, watching her. She looked pale and very young and defenceless, staring out of the window. Much too young. His heart twisted. He wanted to comfort her, hug her like a child, but he knew if he touched her she would move away.

She smiled at him. 'I'm fine. It's all right.'

'It's not all right. There's a lot wrong. Do you think I don't know that? But you won't talk. You won't tell me. Why don't you start your work again?'

'I can't,' she said simply. 'There's nothing there. Only blankness and emptiness. Nothing is real enough to paint.'

'What's the matter, Cathy. Is it me?'

'I just can't seem to get in touch with things again. Nothing is real any more. It's as though I'm in a cage. No, not a cage...a glass case. Like a stuffed bird. I can't break the glass.'

Dev stared at her angrily. 'Not glass, Cathy. *Ice.* To keep me out. To drive me away, so I can't get to you. But listen, girl, you're not going to get away, *ever.*'

Cathy's voice was too high. 'What are you talking about?'

'Just because I don't talk about it like Chris, it doesn't mean I don't know. Connected. For*ever*, Cathy. Give up fighting.'

She shook her head, near to tears, feeling trapped and panicky.

The next day Dev said, casually, too casually, 'I'd like you to come along to our recording sessions, Cathy. Come up to town with us tomorrow.'

She stared at him, surprised. 'But why? What would I do all the time? They go on for hours.'

'Listen. See how we're doing. Make suggestions. Criticise.' Dev's voice was steel under the silk, and she knew he had made up his mind. He drove the knife in deeper. 'You're not doing anything here, are you? Not painting?'

Cathy closed her eyes. 'No.'

Power games, she realised suddenly. Dev didn't need criticism. He was his own worst critic, working meticulously to the highest possible musical standards, to the point where he drove everyone, even Chris, crazy. Dev was choosing this way of showing his power over her, drawing her closer to him and blocking her bid for freedom.

'I'd like your company. It will be really nice having you along.'

She knew he was out-manoeuvring her, but it was difficult to argue. Cathy felt that married partners had every right to ask for each other's support and company. She looked at him despairingly, and Dev smiled back, blandly.

Dev and Chris went to the recording studios most days. Sitting between them in the big car, like someone arrested in a TV thriller, she thought, Cathy went with them.

She had hoped to be allowed to doze on the deep sofas in the reception area while she waited for them, but she found herself in the engineer's control room on a hard chair, listening carefully and trying to understand the complex process of making a new Easy Connection album.

'Come on, Cathy, we're all stuck,' shouted Chris, through the microphone, on the second day. 'What's your idea?'

Cathy flushed as the sound engineer looked sideways at her sceptically. She leaned forward. 'I don't know anything about rock.'

'You know about jazz and the blues. What would B.B. do?'

'Raise the tempo, and let it all go,' she said, smiling. 'Maybe you need a bridge section. Quiet. Gentle.'

'That's it. Easy,' said the sound engineer, surprised. 'A sax?'

'A clarinet I thought,' Cathy said, tentative.

'Ronnie Craig,' said Dev. 'Get on to him, Gil. In Dave Hampton's band. See if he'll do the session for us. He's the best clarinet in the business.'

'They're accepting the suggestion?' Cathy said to the engineer.

'Of course. It's right.' The engineer grinned, his eyes speculative. 'You're not just a pretty face are you? You've also got nice...'

'Keep your thoughts to yourself, Gil,' snapped Dev.

The engineer switched off the intercom. 'Christ, he's jumpy. That's not like him. What's the matter with him?'

'Jealousy,' said Dev, pleasantly, behind him at the door of the booth. 'She's my wife. No funny business or you'll be unfit for work.'

Gil laughed and flapped his hand. 'You know I'm not into girls, *darling*.'

But Dev did not laugh. 'And switch that bloody thing on. I want to know what's happening.'

Cathy laughed aloud, and went on laughing, despite Dev's furious glances. 'You said you'd enjoy having me along,' she said.

At the end of the sessions Cathy was exhausted, longing for the quiet of the barn, but most evenings Dev and Chris relaxed by dropping into one or other of the West End's exclusive and expensive clubs for professional musicians, or taking in a back-stage party after a gig by somebody they knew. They seemed to know everybody.

'I'd like you to meet my friends, Cathy,' Dev said. There seemed to be a great many of them suddenly. He enjoyed showing her off, watching their startled reaction. He had won and he was determined everybody should know it.

They were always the centre of a big noisy group. Dev, Chris, Keith Hurst, sometimes Keith's wife, Lisa, Leo Field, Bill Hopkins, friends like Dave Hampton. Always too, were the hangers-on and any girls they fancied and picked up.

At midnight, Dev and Chris were just beginning the evening, winding down. Their energy seemed inexhaustible. But Cathy felt tired and heavy with her pregnancy. She hated the blaze of publicity and notoriety that surrounded the band wherever they went, the way people turned round and watched them. Every evening in the smoky clubs was an ordeal of gaping, curious faces.

'You're a very trusting lady,' said Chris, lazily, in Cathy's ear one evening. He was lounging back in the darkened booth of the club where they were eating, watching Dev who was dancing with a girl on the tiny dance floor. She had her arms wound round his neck and her body clamped to his all the way down. Dev seemed to be enjoying it. At any rate he was moving his hands up and down her back.

Cathy looked away. Chris' bare arm brushed against hers, and she moved along the seat too quickly, and heard him laugh.

'I notice you never ask him where he's been, what he's been doing, why he's late.'

She smiled slightly. 'I knew before I married him there would be other girls. So long as he doesn't bring them to the house.'

Chris looked at her strangely. 'Your self-esteem is pretty low, Cathy. He was faithful to his last lady. He never looked at anyone else. But she was insanely jealous of him. Dev loved that. He thought it meant she really cared. He was wrong.'

Cathy shrugged, trying to ignore the depression, which was spreading rapidly through her.

'I know people go off and leave you. Chris, I'm *trying* to be trusting. What are you implying anyway? That he's found another girl already?'

Chris nodded to the dance floor. 'There's a lot of temptation in the music business, Cathy. A married man walks a tightrope. You'll have to fight for him if you want him.'

Cathy shook her head. 'I'm not competing, trying crafty women's tricks. I think everybody should have the right to choose freely. It's up to Dev.'

What was Chris trying to tell her? Cathy felt tense and upset, and when Dev came off the floor, his arm still around the girl, and asked if she wanted to dance with him, she shook her head and danced with Chris instead.

It sometimes seemed to Cathy that her depression and weariness had become a more or less permanent state. But when she began to feel physically ill – not just exhausted and heavy – but full of odd pains and queasiness, she became very frightened. Was something going wrong with the baby? The idea that she might now lose it appalled her. Panic-stricken, she evaded the security men and went to see Dr. Eliot in the village.

He was reassuring. Everything seemed to be going well. She must go on eating sensibly and rest in the afternoons. Cathy smiled grimly, remembering the noise and frenzy of the clubs and the appalling curries Dev and Chris sent out for in the studio breaks.

She was not sleeping well either. She had begun to have nightmares, full of guilt and anxiety about the baby being born with terrible deformities. How could he be healthy and whole when he had been conceived in such a way? But she could not bring herself to talk about the nightmares with anybody.

The noise and confusion of the house woke her early and she could not sleep again. Sometimes she felt lightheaded with the need for sleep, but Dev did not seem to notice or care.

When she told him she needed to rest and ought to come home when the sessions ended, he smiled nastily. 'Wriggling again, Cathy?'

Dev bought clothes for her. He knew exactly what Cathy ought to wear. His interest in fashion was much greater than her own and he liked spending money. In the evening he loved girls in thirties-style dresses, in clinging black crepe or pink silk chiffons, low-cut, with beads and fringes.

Cathy hated them. She felt strange in them, too undressed, too sexy.

'Please, Dev, don't go on buying these things,' Cathy said. 'I don't feel like myself. And it's a waste of money. I won't be able to get into them in a few weeks. These low tops... I mean, I'm getting bigger there and...'

'I noticed,' Dev said smiling. 'You look fabulous. Titania and Dolly Parton. We'll go to Rick's party tonight after the recording session. Wear the one with the long silver fringe.'

Cathy tried to shrug away her growing anger and resentment. She tried to tell herself it was Dev's way of showing care and concern, but deep down she felt as if he was playing with her, like a toy. Sometimes she wondered what would happen when he got bored and wanted a new toy. But he was showing no signs of boredom yet. He insisted on shopping in Bond Street for expensive jewellery, which offended Cathy's political feelings, and for impossibly high-heeled sandals, which she found difficult to wear. A hairdresser came, and, directed by Dev, piled her long hair up on to her head, in a cascade of shining curls.

'Can't *you* stop him, Chris?' Cathy said, desperately, at last. 'I feel like a Sindy doll.'

Chris laughed softly. 'You're beautiful, Cathy.'

He stood very close and his fingers drifted gently down over the curves of her cheek and lips, down the smooth swell of her breasts, along the line of the low-cut dress. She stood away from him, trying to breath normally, but her heart was banging so loudly, he must know how aroused she was.

'If you were mine, Cathy, you wouldn't worry about clothes.'

She looked at him uncertainly, saw his eyes, hot and smiling dangerously and went scarlet. Why couldn't she learn to take Chris' sexual innuendoes without reacting? She walked away, pretending she hadn't understood.

'You wouldn't be sleeping alone, either. Dev must be rationing himself, like a drunk in a whisky factory.'

She slammed the door and stood against it, aroused and furious with herself. A simple touch, a few sentences and her body was way out of her control. How did they do it? Dev and Chris were the only men who had ever had this effect on her and she couldn't handle either of them.

She took a deep breath, realising suddenly, that if Chris ever found out the truth, there would be nothing to hold him off at all.

Cathy felt disorientated and unreal. The girl reflected in the mirror looked fabulous. The heavily beaded dresses clung revealingly to her. Her grey-violet eyes, darkened by fatigue looked enormous and other worldly in her pale skin. She looked fragile and sexily seductive at the same time.

But what had happened to *herself*, that other, untidy, r*eal* girl, laughing and alive? The girl with paint smears on her face and her shirt sleeves rolled above her elbows? Sometimes it seemed she could not remember who she really was. Dev was making her over into his own fantasy image.

A fantasy, it seemed, shared by a lot of other people.

To her horror, the media had caught up with her again. She fitted in very nicely between the famous footballer's wife, and the latest television celebrity. The way she looked, her youth, the romance of her marriage to a hell-raising rock star, and something else, indefinable, had caught the public imagination. Increasingly there were items about her in the gossip columns. Where she went, what she wore, who she spoke to, danced with, seemed to interest an astonishing number of people.

Dev and Chris were amused. 'You'll get used to it.'

'No I won't! I'll never get used to it.' She tried to explain, haltingly, her horror of living in a blaze of publicity that they took for granted.

Dev said, impatiently, 'I don't know why these people worry you. All you have to do is smile, wave your hand and run for the limo. They just want to look at you. Touch you maybe.' He grinned. 'Hsien.'

'No, that's you and Chris. They look at me to find all the worst faults, wondering why you married me.'

Dev lounging on the hall sofa, next to Chris, laughed aloud. 'You think that's what the guys are thinking, Chris?'

Chris smiled slowly, letting his glance move over her body. 'It's not what I think when I look at her, Dev.'

Cathy turned away, angry and hurt at their cat and mouse double act, their lack of understanding and support.

'Mike,' she said, desperately, to Easy Connection's Publicity Manager, 'Do I really have to do this interview for *Female*? This is our home. I wanted it to be private.'

Dev said, irritated, 'It's just a little interview. Nothing to get hung up about. They'll ask you what I eat for breakfast and what I wear in bed.'

'How do I know?' snapped Cathy, furiously, and saw Chris' light eyes, fixed, suddenly intent on her. She swung away, the tears standing in her eyes. Her voice rose. 'Isn't there *anywhere* we can be free without all these people coming around? I can't even go out and buy a tube of toothpaste now without a gang of people following me. I just can't stand much more of it. Don't you understand?'

To her surprise, Bill Hopkins came to her support.

'Cancel it, Mike.'

'But Bill, you know...'

'Forget it,' he said, tersely. 'It's too early. Cathy isn't ready for any of this. Remember Dev last year? This marriage has got to work. You want the Connection breaking up? Dev breaking up?'

Mike said, puzzled, 'What's that got to do with...'
'Think about it, Mike. And cancel that interview.'

The interview was cancelled, but free-lance photographers lay in wait wherever she went – venues, restaurants, clubs – chasing her car from place to place to get the latest story, the exclusive picture. It was worse, much worse, than it had been in Hamilton Square, and it drove Cathy frantic. The more the media spotlighted her, the more trapped she was feeling, the last of her personal freedom draining away.

'Please, Dev, can't we come home early tonight? I don't want to go to this première. I need some sleep.'

Dev said, icily, 'You can't creep into a hole and hide, Cathy. They won't go away.'

Cathy said, wearily, 'I'm just tired Dev. I need the rest.'

'Maybe you ought to be in a nursing home.'

'All right, I'll come to the première if it's that important.'

It was dangerously easy now to give in to Dev without argument. She felt so miserable and tired. It seemed that they were hardly ever at home. Every minute of her day was taken up by Dev and Chris. There was no time to talk privately. There was no time to think, or find her way back to her real self. There was no time to find her way back to her painting. Dev had taken over. Her buried anger and resentment grew like fungus in a dark place, draining her vital energy.

Chapter Six

Cathy knew she could not go on much longer. She felt very ill. The attention of the media, the long hours in the studio, the interminable parties, her efforts to meet Dev's expectations had affected her badly. She slept fitfully, and the nightmares about the baby got worse. She could hardly eat. The canvas on her easel remained white and mocking. She was frightened that one day, the hate and anger inside her would break free and destroy everything, like a flow of lava.

'We can't go on like this,' Dev said, coming unexpectedly into the barn one morning. 'What's the matter with you?'

Cathy struggled to her feet. 'I'm sorry. You're waiting to go. I thought we didn't have to go in to town today.'

'We don't. I just wanted to see you. Talk to you. You're like a ghost. You hardly talk. You just aren't there half the time. I want you to tell me what's wrong.'

'What's the point? You don't listen when I do.'

'I'm listening now.'

'I've told you, lots of times, but you don't understand. Sometimes you don't even *hear*. The things I think are important you dismiss. We're so far apart you could be a Martian. Oh, what's the use.'

'I said, talk, Cathy.'

She took a long breath. 'I'm not painting – that's the first thing. I don't paint because I want to Dev. I paint because I have to. If I don't, I get sick. My brain and my soul get sick. I'm sick *now*. Do you understand that? You say – what does it matter? I don't need the money. I think, deep down, you're pleased I'm not painting, I can concentrate on you instead.

'There's no time for me to paint now anyway. We're always going somewhere, trivial *useless* activities, filling up my time and my mind, so I can't hear myself inside.

Then I'm dreadfully tired and don't feel well. Sometimes it's like that in the first months of a pregnancy. I'm supposed to rest, but there's no let up. We're out till three every night practically. I can't sleep properly. I...I have these nightmares. If I say anything you say I'm wriggling out of the marriage.

'I know you're not happy either. But I don't know what you want from me. I come out with you, talk to your friends nicely, I wear the clothes you choose. I don't ask for your time or attention. I don't interfere. I keep out of your business. I don't ask prying questions. I don't stop you going where you want, when you want...'

Dev stared at her. 'That's right, Cathy. You do all those things.'

'But it's not enough is it? I suppose it's the sex. I told you it would be no good.'

He said impatiently, 'Forget the sex. Okay, it's a strain and I want you, but that's not the problem. I can get sex anywhere.'

'Then it's *me*, isn't it? You've found out you don't really like the kind of person I am.'

'Are you crazy?'

'Ever since we got married you've been trying to change me. You didn't like my clothes and you didn't like my hairstyle, and you didn't like the way I feel about money. You don't even respect my opinions. You know how I feel about killing animals for fur coats, and wearing expensive jewellery when so many people are starving, but you make me wear them all the same.'

Dev said, appalled, 'Cathy, you've got it wrong. I don't want to change you. You're so beautiful I just want to make you even more beautiful.'

'So you can show me off to your friends like a new Maserati? I don't want to be a beautiful object, Dev. I want to be *me*. Wear the things I like.'

'Why do you keep bringing up these stupid minor matters when we're trying to have a serious discussion?'

'There you are, you see?' Her eyes blazed with resentment. '*You* think they're stupid, but to me they're really important. They're about my freedom, my independence, my privacy, my politics. How I think and feel. You ride over my opinions, not even noticing them. I know I'm young, but you smile, you pat me like a poodle and forget I've said anything. You're trying to take me over completely. Get into my mind and tell me what to think.

'If you want to use big concepts, Dev, I'm not *free*. I feel trapped and everything is closing in. I feel like that song – someone is watching me.'

'*Watching* you?' he said, incredulously.

'All the time. You come poking about in my bedroom, my studio, looking at things, asking questions. Trying to get into my head. I don't come poking into your brain and feelings. I don't try to push into your private space!' Her voice rose hysterically. 'I tell you I don't know what you want from me.'

He took a deep breath. 'Cathy, hasn't it struck you that's just what I *do* want? I *want* you in my private space. I want you to get into my head and know everything about me. I want to come into a room and have you come running, wanting to know what I've been doing. I want you to worry if I don't come home. I want to be so close we're like one person. Total intimacy. That's how I want marriage to be.'

Cathy could not conceal her horror. 'But I've got to have some privacy. I've got to feel free. I can't be as close as that to anyone.'

They stared at each other, silent, aware of the chasm opening between them.

'Not ever, Cathy?'

The silence lengthened.

'No, I don't think so...Oh how do I know?' She looked out of the window at the distant hills. 'Maybe. If I trusted them. Loved them.'

Dev moved away quickly. At the door he stopped and turned back.

'Cathy – that painting of the tree and the stream. Where is it?'

'What painting?'

His eyes narrowed. He said, slowly, spacing the words, 'The painting you were doing the day we met down by the stream. The old tree and the dark water. The one I offered to buy.'

'Why do you want it?' she asked, uneasily.

'I like it. I want to hang it in my room.'

'I haven't got it.'

'But we brought all your stuff down here from Hamilton Square. You must have it. You've not sold it!'

'I don't remember.'

'I suppose Caleb Crow took it,' he said, annoyed. 'I'll get on to him and have him send it back.' He turned to the door again.

'Caleb hasn't got it. I threw it away.'

'The reason we met at all. *You threw it away.*'

Cathy put her hand on her stomach. 'You think I want to be reminded of that day? I've already got a souvenir, Dev.'

A muscle moved in Dev's throat. His eyes were too bright. Cathy looked back at him, knowing he could read her rage and resentment, and not caring.

Afterwards she realised that this was when things got so much worse between them, and the quarrels started. Dev pursued her ruthlessly with sarcasm, wounding remarks, verbal attacks, punching through the barrier of ice to bring her alive and make her notice him. Sometimes she flared into an incandescent fury, which left her sick and ashamed and feeling physically ill, as she remembered the break-up of her parents' marriage.

And always there was Chris, mocking and amused, his sensual body sprawled on the sofas, watching them. Was it her imagination that there were always more rows, more arguments, when Chris was around?

'I'm not going!' Cathy burst out. 'I feel heavy and awkward and stupid. Everybody staring at me. I'm staying here and going to bed early for once.'

Dev's eyes were hard. 'Listen, I kept my part of the bargain. If I'm not getting you in bed, at least you'll come out with me when I say so.'

The attack sent colour burning into Cathy's cheeks and silenced her. Behind her, she heard Chris laugh. She spun round and stared directly into his light eyes, full of unholy laughter. He had come into the garden room so quietly he must have overheard, but he did not seem surprised. *He already knew.* Dev had told him after all. The knowledge hit her painfully. Betrayal of trust – the worst crime. Cathy felt cold and hopeless.

Chris stretched out casually on one of the leather sofas, and put his grubby trainers on one of his own light sculpture tables. He looked over her head, grinning at Dev, enjoying the quarrel.

'Not much of a trade, Dev. You must be slipping.'

She ignored Chris and tried to keep her voice low and even, unemotional. 'I thought you wanted this baby, Dev. I'm telling you truly – I can't keep up. I can't go on. I need some rest.'

'You're just making excuses, Cathy,' Chris said, dryly. 'You don't want to be with us.'

Dev said, his voice hard and vicious, 'She's trying to get away from me.'

Chris laughed. 'Maybe she's frightened you'll get drunk and affectionate. You might forget your promise and put your hands on her.'

Cathy said, tightly, 'Does he have to be here all the time, even in a private conversation?'

'What do we have to say to each other that's so private?' Dev said, bitterly. 'Don't worry, sweetheart. It's a woman I want in my bed. A warm loving woman. Not a pale ghost.'

Cathy said, hoarse with rage, 'Who turned me into a ghost? Not a ghost, a *dolly*. I'm so tired I can hardly stand up and you're blaming me. I'm your creation, Dev. I'm what you wanted. A porcelain dolly, without opinions, saying 'Da-da, da-da' when she's squeezed. You're just like your father. You've walked all over me.'

Dev's eyes glittered. 'You didn't have to marry me. It was your choice.'

Her pent-up bitterness burst. 'Girls don't have much choice, Dev. How could I get a job with a baby needing to be looked after? What else was there? You need to have money to walk away. I wish they told you that in school.'

Dev took a long breath. 'Okay. If it's so bad – there's the door, you can walk out whenever you want. You're free.'

There was an uncanny silence. Cathy stared at him and then at the door. To walk out. To go through, get her bag and basket and walk out – go back to College. A small, quiet room somewhere. In control of her own life. She felt sick with the intensity of her longing. Her muscles stiffened, ready to stand up...

And then, suddenly, the baby inside her, kicked, and brought back reality. Nothing had changed. *A con trick.* She glanced at Dev angrily and surprised a look of such naked fear that she had to look away again. It made her feel more angry and guilty too. 'And what about *this?* ' She pointed her shaking finger at her stomach. 'What about the darling little son you wanted so much?'

'You can take him with you!'

Cathy laughed. 'That's right, so I could. I thought we'd get to that kind of blackmail sooner or later. How can a woman with a child be free? You trapped me, Dev. But that's how you see love, isn't it? You even told me. 'Love is a rat-trap,' you said, 'And you can't get out.' But that's not love. That's imprisonment. Love should mean more freedom, exploring new things. And you needn't tell me I've been reading *Sweet Dreams.* If it isn't like that I don't want to know. Who wants to live their life imprisoned in a box?'

'A *cushioned* box, Cathy,' Dev said. 'Wall to wall wealth. A lot of women would like it. Care, concern, being looked after. No hard decisions. Love. Security.'

'Security! Don't make me laugh. With your kind of reputation?'

Dev said, dangerously, 'What about the love, Cathy?'

'You don't love *me*, Dev. You love the thing you made, a pretty dolly in a cushioned box saying 'Da-da'.' She shivered. 'A corpse in a coffin.'

Dev got up. He let his glance move over her body, suggestive and insulting. He said, viciously, 'At least I could take dolly to bed with me,' and walked out, slamming the door.

'Oh dear,' said Chris, softly. 'You shouldn't have mentioned his father. He's got a thing about his father. Are you sure you don't want him, Cathy? Not to worry, there are plenty of girls hanging around the studios. I thought he was giving the media rep the come-on yesterday.'

He put his hands behind his fair hair and leaned back, smiling at her. 'So you're hanging loose, baby. I've wasted an awful lot of time, but I'll be moving a lot closer now.'

Cathy stared at him, frightened. Involuntarily she wondered what it would be like to be Chris' lover and went a fiery red, feeling her body react. He threw back his head and laughed aloud.

'Very, *very*, nice!' he said.

Cathy went up to her room quickly and let the tears come at last. The marriage was falling apart with humiliating speed, even faster than her worse fears. She felt totally alone and helpless.

At last she fell into a heavy sleep, woke dazed, and could not find the strength to get out of bed, or eat the food Mrs. Kaye brought on a tray. There was blood, a frightening amount, staining the sheets.

Dev called in a doctor immediately. Not comfortable Dr. Eliot is the village, but an eminent gynaecologist, who arrived in a Rolls Royce, gave her an injection and pills and said she was suffering from exhaustion, stress and anaemia. She must have bed rest for a week and complete quiet thereafter. Nutritious food. Extra vitamins. Iron injections. She could easily lose the baby.

'Burning the candle, young lady,' he said, disapprovingly. 'Burning the candle!'

'I'm sorry, Cathy,' Dev said, after he had gone. He looked shaken. 'I didn't understand. And Chris was sure you were just...'

She turned her head away into the pillow, despairing. Perhaps it would be better for them all if she did miscarry. It would solve everything. She would be free to go, and Dev could find his warm loving woman, and the baby wouldn't grow up into a hell of quarrelling parents. She spoke the thought aloud, but the idea of the baby not being born at all caused her such a pang of anguish that she closed her eyes and did not notice Dev's icy rage.

The next morning, when he was not around, she got up carefully and slowly, like an invalid, and went to sit in the barn. It was chilly there, but she felt better. The walls were too thick for the noise and confusion of the house to penetrate. It was very peaceful. She looked out across the green meadows and eventually, sighing with relief, she wrapped herself in her duvet and fell asleep on the old divan.

She slept, more or less continuously, and forced herself to eat the special meals Mrs. Kaye made. At the end of the week the specialist came again. The bleeding had stopped and the baby was safe, providing rest and care continued.

'Too bad, Cathy,' Dev said, ironically, leaning against her bedroom door. 'It was a good try, though.'

Her relief and pleasure slid away, as she saw his eyes. *'A good try?'*

'You were supposed to be in bed. You think I don't know you've spent all the time *up*, out there in the barn?'

It was a moment before she understood. 'You mean you think – you think I was trying to bring on a miscarriage?'

'What else?'

'The barn,' she said, with difficulty. 'It was quiet. I could sleep. It was better.'

'Yeah?' He looked around the luxurious bedroom derisively.

'But he's alive. I can feel him move. You really think I'd try to kill him *now*?' she said disbelievingly.

'You thought it was a good idea a week ago.'

'I didn't say that! You don't understand.'

'You wanted an abortion once.'

'Can't you see that was different?'

The shock hit her. He really thought she was capable of killing the baby. She tried to hold back the outraged anger that was threatening to overwhelm her. 'He's over six months old. Able to live on his own. You're saying I'm a murderess.'

'You never wanted him.'

Cathy slid off the bed and stood up. She clasped her hands to stop them shaking, the rage flaring inside her. 'All right. I didn't want the baby. But *I* decided not to have an abortion. *I* decided I would have the baby. Not you. Don't try to spread your poisonous guilt on me. It was your fault I nearly lost the baby. You didn't worry about a miscarriage when you were dragging me around to boost your ego with your friends and show your power over me.'

Dev was ashen. 'Cathy...'

'Why should I want *your* baby, Dev? To be a mother to a baby made in violence and fear and hate? I wanted to be free. I wanted to work. I never wanted to be a mother at all. I never wanted the responsibility...'

'Or the loving,' Dev said, his eyes black with anger. 'You don't want to love the baby and you don't want him to love you. You can't reach out to anybody, not even a baby.'

'How can I?' Cathy said, jerkily, her voice trembling. 'You can only love if you're free. You took away my freedom and my painting...Before I came here...I was all right. I could give people my love through my painting...'

'Well, you can't give anybody anything at all now,' Dev said, jeering. 'Not even a painting.'

Chapter Seven

The Easy Connection Far East tour was starting off with a single concert at Wembley for the English fans. Tickets went on sale by postal ballot and the black market price soared to an all-time high. The final preparations for the tour went ahead with long frenetic hours of rehearsal.

'You'll be there, Cathy?' Dev asked, abruptly, sounding uncertain. It was the first time he had asked her to go anywhere for several weeks.

Since the big quarrel, they had hardly spoken. On the surface they were polite, almost friendly, each drawing back, shaken, afraid of re-opening the deep wounds. But poison lay in the wounds and they were not healing. Cathy felt hopeless, too resentful to try to do anything about Dev's hurt and misunderstanding. It was a long time since he had touched her or sat with his arm around her.

Dev looked grim and strained, and drank increasing amounts of vodka. According to the roadies, when he was out of hearing, he was being the difficult superstar, a prey to perfectionism and unreasonable ideas, demanding a standard nobody thought could be achieved.

Dev said, 'It's our last night, Cathy.'

A concession – or an appeal? Cathy could not guess. She hesitated, not wanting concessions.

'You've never seen one of our big gigs,' Chris said. 'You'd enjoy it. They're spectacular.'

Cathy said to Dev, 'Do you want me there?'

He stared at her. 'Of course I bloody want you there. What do you think!'

'All right, then I'd like to come.'

'You'll need a stage pass.'

'I'd be in the way. I'd rather be in the audience.'

He said exasperated, 'Are you crazy? You'd go under in the rush.'

Chris laughed. 'They'd have your clothes off you as souvenirs.'

Cathy flushed. 'They wouldn't know me.'

He laughed again. 'They'd know you all right. You're one of us now, Cathy. Part of rock history. Our fans have got a word for it – *connected*.'

'I'm not a fan.'

'Wait till you see Chris strutting his stuff,' Dev grinned at him. 'You'll be asking for his autograph.'

Chris smiled into her eyes. 'Cathy can have whatever she wants from me.'

The concert was as spectacular as they had promised. From the moment Keith Hurst's drums had beaten out a crescendo of ear-splitting sound against the full-throated roar of welcome from the packed audience, the atmosphere was electric with the feeling of a big occasion.

From a silver spider-web grid high above the band huge mirror screens hung. The screens moved and revolved in the flashing laser light, reflecting and enlarging the band together and separately as they too moved about the stage, so that it was filled with figures, some real, some ghosts, which grew to giant size and shrank again, blanking out mysteriously as the screens turned. Four hundred motorised lamps throbbed rhythmically from the lighting rig, and it was difficult to see what was real and what was a silver and rainbow dream. The sound crashed out clear and perfect on seventy thousand watts.

Dev prowled the stage, dangerous as a big cat, nervous tension and high energy pulsing around him, almost tangible, as his guitar soared and sobbed above the heavy beat.

And there was Chris, crouching, arching, using his voice like an instrument, powerful and rasping, biting into the lyrics, sometimes soft and infinitely tender, sometimes loud, brash, arrogant.

Cathy was stunned. She had heard Chris sing the blues at a private party, but this was different again. His personal magnetism spun a net around the vast arena, and held the audience fixed and hypnotised, as he played upon their emotions. She understood at last the fervour of the Easy Connection fans, and why the Connection was considered to be one of the finest of all rock bands. The musicians slotted together, each powerful and dramatic in their own right. Keith Hurst on drums, Leo Field on bass. They had been together a long time, and Chris had said once that they were very, *very* good. She had thought he was boasting, but she knew now that he had merely spoken the truth.

On this tour they had, in addition, a keyboards player, synthesisers, a variety of electronic effects, and a second drummer – to reproduce the rich experimental sound they had used on their *Head Start* album, Dev had told her.

Waiting to go on he had been chalk white, keyed to an unbearable pitch, and Chris, his eyes dilated, had been laughing too often and too quickly.

They were wearing tight, silver leather trousers, Dev in a sleeveless silken vest sewn with mirror discs, flashing in the lights and Chris in a silver leather waistcoat, open, with an antique silver dagger hanging against his bare skin.

'It's really dangerous,' Cathy had said, horrified. 'You could cut yourself.' The point of the knife brushing along the taut stomach muscles made her shiver. She looked away and Dev laughed. 'He does sometimes. On purpose. It drives the fans bananas.'

'Like this,' Chris watched her with his light, unreadable eyes. Deliberately he drew the tip of the knife along his skin leaving a thin red thread, beaded with blood. Cathy cried out, then before she realised his intention he caught her hand. There was a smarting at her wrist and the tiny spurt of blood was pressed into his own, her hand held hard against him.

'Are you completely out of your mind, Chris?' She tore her hand away, furious and upset.

Dev and Chris were laughing, amused at her over-reaction.

'You're a maniac!'

'Come on, Chris. It's time. We're on.'

Chris watched him walk away and looked at Cathy. He had stopped laughing. 'A blood wedding,' he said softly.

Cathy was as near to the stage as Dev could get her, perched reluctantly on one of the packing cases standing ready to be loaded into the big trailers outside. Perspiring roadies rolled their cables and ducked across the stage, grinning at her. Dev's personal roadie, Cal Bowman, bent over equipment, smiled at her tiredly, and Cathy guessed that Dev had been giving him a hard time.

From where she was sitting she could see the front rows of fans, standing, stretching long silver banners across the rows which they held high in the wild waves of applause, as they swayed and sang along to the rocking rhythms of their favourite Connection songs. Most of the audience were in their late teens and twenties and male. Easy Connection was no teeny-bopper band.

The concert was continuous for the first forty minutes – one song after another, all Easy Connection classics, famous chart hits. They recalled memories of previous concerts, building the excitement and nostalgia.

At the first break the musicians used towels and drank cans of beer, and Chris' voice, big over the sound stacks, disembodied, said, 'Glad to see you again. Hope you're enjoying yourselves,' and was answered by a happy uproar of cheers, shrieks and whistles.

'Here's something new.'

He sang two songs from their latest album, and then, grinning wickedly at Cathy, he began to sing *Cathy Sleeping*. It was full of strange wailing rhythms from the synths and the guitars, with a slow, irregular drum beating, throbbing into the blood. Chris' voice was sensual, the words shockingly erotic.

'Half our new album is about you,' Dev had once said. Cathy stared at her hands, scarlet with embarrassment, conscious of the grinning roadies.

And then, at last, it was over and suddenly the atmosphere had changed. Now it had a charged intensity, almost serious. Chris sang the most famous of all the Connection's revolutionary songs, *Devil Runs the Streets*.

The audience were waiting now. The lights had dimmed and silver spotlights shone on each of the members of the band. Dev and Chris were shoulder to shoulder at the very edge of the stage, near to the reaching fans.

Chris said, 'You know that song. The others were from the new album, not released yet. It's called *Message from Annarres*...Annarres is an anarchist planet. The message remains the same...FREEDOM!'

Excitement rose and fountained. It was the beginning of the famous chant done at every Easy Connection concert.

'Freedom!' The crowd roared back, ecstatic.

'Truth.'

'Truth!' chanted the crowd.

'Independence.'

'Independence!'

'Courage.'

'Courage!'

'LOVE.'

'LOVE!'

'LOVE AND FREEDOM.'

'LOVE...FREEEEEEEEEEDOM!'

Then an ear-splitting yell, band and audience together, a forest of linked hands raised over their heads, 'CONNECTED!'

It was like a tribal chant or a kind of religious oath. Despite herself Cathy felt moved and shaken. She felt tears in her eyes. It was so stupid. How could you be free *and* connected? How could the fans let their best feelings be cynically exploited by a band like Easy Connection? She looked accusingly towards Dev, and found he had turned away from Chris and was staring directly at her, challengingly, his eyes glittering.

Did they really believe it? Had they really lived their lives according to the Message? It was true they were free. They went ahead and did what they wanted. They did not cover up or compromise. They faced attack with humour and courage.

But if they only believed in freedom for themselves, did that count?

She realised then, suddenly, with a rush of understanding that you had to follow the Message for yourself. No one helped you to be free. No one helped you to be courageous. You had to do it by yourself. It was no use blaming other people. That's what they meant by personal responsibility. If you were a girl it was very, very difficult. They didn't want you to be free.

Cathy stared blindly into the brilliant light. Truth. Love. Independence. Courage. Freedom. Each word was stamped into her brain.

She had given them all up.

She had surrendered them one by one and run for cover, looking for someone to look after her like a little girl. She had sold out, even her talent betrayed, traded for security. No wonder she had turned into a dolly. She had turned *herself* into a dolly.

Her heart felt as though it might easily burst, as a chaotic flood of disgust, regret, and finally, anguish, at what she had done, poured over her. Failure and defeat at the very beginning of her life.

She found she was on her feet, needing to move, shaking with tension. She spun round, but it was darker now, the lights pulsing hot red and magenta, and she stumbled over a lead. A man waved at her frantically to keep still, and she became aware that Chris was singing again. *I Put a Spell on You,* the old Screamin' J. Hawkins song.

He was stalking the forestage alone, his head thrown back, his maleness blatant and arrogant, his eyes half-closed, holding the audience. Chris had always seemed so relaxed and casual compared to Dev, but now she realised she was seeing the real Chris Carter, his sexuality and magnetism usually carefully tamped down, bursting into flame, igniting the audience. He was almost sinister in his power.

Put a spell on you
Because you're mine...

He circled the stage, crouching in the brilliant red spot, using his dagger like a witch doctor, and pointing directing at her.

I put a spell on you
Because you're mine.

Cathy shivered uncontrollably, the hair lifting on her neck, fixed by the pointing dagger. His voice was low, menacing, and the huge audience was suddenly stilled.

I said, watch out. I ain't lyin'.

At the end of the song, the applause was thunderous. There was an uproar of calls for an encore, but Chris walked off the stage abruptly and Dev went directly into his solo instrumental, *Bro' Death,* a display of his virtuoso guitar playing.

Chris' ash blonde hair was dark with perspiration dripping down his neck. He was breathing fast and his eyes were wild. He drank two cans of Carlsberg straight down, and stood behind Cathy, towelling himself, watching Dev.

'He's incredible tonight. Better than ever. This is his *Freebird*. Only better. You know the *Freebird* guitar break? Lynard Skynard?'

She shook her head, not want to talk, lost in the cascade of sound.

Dev was concentrating. His face was expressionless, as though carved in marble, beautiful and pure. The low slow thrumming, the single slow crying of his guitar, had become the sweeping passionate sound of wanting, desperate regrets, failed hopes.

Cathy was caught, drowning in emotion, because he seemed to be expressing all she was feeling tonight. She was not even aware, at first, that Chris had moved closer and put his arms around her, holding her back close against him.

'Cathy.'

His lips were warm on the nape of her neck. He was kissing the line of her shoulders, her ears, and his long fingers were moving on her breasts, feeling through the thin fabric. Shocked, she found her body aroused, burning with electrical fire. She tugged his hands away and tried to twist out of his grasp. 'Let go.'

But he pulled her back against the pile of cases and kissed her mouth open.

Then suddenly, Gregg Fisher, Chris' personal roadie, was there, tapping him on the shoulder.

'Chris – you're on again. You want the bag?'

Chris was breathing raggedly. 'No...Yes.'

Gregg produced a paper bag and turned his back shielding it from view as Chris bent his head, inhaled the powder and walked back into the spinning, flaring lights, the mad cheering for Dev's solo.

Cathy tried not to look at Gregg. She took a deep breath. 'All right?'

'Yes. Thanks for...Thanks.'

'No bother.' He wasn't about to tell her that part of his job was trying to keep Chris out of trouble.

He said, quietly, 'It doesn't mean anything. He's stoned. On a really big high tonight.'

'I know.' She drew another deep, shaky breath.

'And going on the road tomorrow...'

'Yes. It's all right.'

He grinned at her impudently, flicking back his straight waist-length hair in its sweatband. 'Anyone would, if they got the chance. No need to tell Dev?'

The colour left Cathy's cheeks. 'No!'

'Start of the tour. Black eyes make a bad impression.'

'They *fight?*'

'It's happened.' He didn't want to remember the raw brutality of that fight and Chris' broken rib.

'I won't say anything.'

'Cheers.' He turned away, feeling better. Chris must be crazy drunk, making an open pass at Dev's woman on the side stage, even if she did look straight off page three. Not a trouble maker, though, thank God.

'Gregg, is there any paper anywhere? Big paper. I want to draw.'

'*Now?*' He looked at her and shrugged. 'Used stuff, maybe. Poster backs. Wrapping paper.'

'*Anything.* It doesn't matter. And chalk?'

'Sure, plenty of chalk.' He looked at her curiously, but she did not notice. She was staring at the stage, her eyes wide open, strange.

She climbed higher on the packing cases out of the way of the cables and working roadies, to get a clearer view and in a few minutes Gregg put a pile of unused posters and some dark grey wrapping paper next to her. He closed her fingers around some chalk and a thick felt-tip pen. Not taking her eyes off Dev and Chris, Cathy said, 'You're a genius, Gregg. I could hug you.'

'You want I should end up in hospital?'

Cathy laughed and Gregg ducked away.

Dev and Chris were close together now, face to face, staring at each other, a counterpoint of guitar and voice. The intense silver spotlights had gathered about them glancing off their clothes and the spinning background of mirrors like a prism, locking them into a prison of scintillating rays. Their faces and hair looked silver too, mask-like, only their eyes seemed human, feverish and brilliant.

They were feeding on the excitement, the love rising almost tangibly from the audience. Plugged in. No. *Connected.* Their word. They were making a main connection, but even drugs couldn't give such a high. She understood now. For this they went on working to exhaustion, tour after tour. Album after album. Dev and Chris weren't free after all. They were addicted. No matter how much money they had, this is what they needed. They were trapped in the silver spotlights. Silver space lords, unable to fly.

She used the top of the packing case next to her as a drawing board, the biro from her bag, the pencil from her diary, the felt pen and the chalk, singly and superimposed on another, *anything* to get her vision down, pushing away each drawing impatiently, as she finished. Her hand, slow and uncertain at first, began to move faster and faster. Some were simple drawings, the line of a thigh, the turn of a shoulder; others were more detailed studies of the interlocking rays, the stage movement, the frenzy, the light and dark, the *connection.*

She was unaware of the time passing, only dimly aware of the music as song followed song, and the excitement built to an unbearable pitch. But she saw, and drew, the fans, agonised and entranced, struggling against the thin line of security men. She saw too, the exhaustion of the band, as they got through a fourth or fifth encore, before coming to a halt, physically unable to play another note, grinning at the frantic fans, cheering and cheering.

Cathy glanced at her watch and saw that they had been playing for over three hours. Even the roadies and stage hands were clapping as they came off, waving at the audience. Chris was laughing like a maniac and Dev looked wild and reckless, the adrenalin still flowing.

Cathy shrank back, hoping he had forgotten she was there, knowing how unpredictable and dangerous he was in this kind of mood. But he reached up for her, knowing exactly where she was, swung her down into his arms and kissed her hard on the mouth. She could feel his physical arousal, and frightened, struggled away from him. He held her, kissed her again, laughing, and swept her along with them to the dressing rooms backstage, already full of food, drink, famous faces, and loud with laughter and jokes.

Cal Bowman, Dev's roadie, with another three hours of the back-breaking get-out in front of him, straightened and put his heel on his cigarette. He picked up the scattered drawings, rolled them carefully into another poster and took them out to Dev's waiting limousine. She might ask who had rescued them, or more likely she wouldn't. He had been watching her all evening between jobs. He had fallen for her, crazily, like a teenager, at the Farm, much to Dev and Chris' malicious amusement. But Cathy didn't even know he was alive.

He wondered what the hell Chris had been playing at. In all the years of being on the road with him, working so closely, he had never seen Chris look like he had holding Cathy. He thought he'd buy Gregg a good long beer when he got the chance.

Chapter Eight

'Cathy.'

Dev was standing inside her door.

Cathy groaned and turned over. She lifted herself on one elbow and stared at the illuminated dial of her bedside clock. Nearly three thirty. They had got back late. It had taken hours to get away from the back-stage party.

'What is it?' Half asleep still, she stared towards him, a dark figure silhouetted against the light from the hall outside. Then, suddenly, she understood and came fully awake. Her heart beat painfully in her throat.

'I-Is something wrong?'

He shut the door and came across the room through the pools of silver moonlight spreading on the carpet from the big windows. He stood next to her looking down, silver again, metallic in the bright light. She gripped the sheet to her tightly.

'I can't sleep.'

'I'll get you some tablets...' She began to get out of bed.

He pushed her back. 'No.'

'Dev...'

'Cathy, I'm going away tomorrow. For three months. I won't see you for so long...I can't stand it. It's *agony*. You've got to come with me.'

'You know I can't. The baby is due soon. Please, it's late. It's too late to talk.'

'I don't want to talk.'

There was a give-away silence. Cathy felt all her muscles tighten. 'Dev...we *can't*. It'd harm the baby.'

But Dev pulled the cover away from her hands and moved in beside her. His naked body was warm and muscular. He put his arms around her and held her cuddled against him.

'Dev, I'm frightened. I'm not ready. You said you would wait...The baby...'

'You're my wife, Cathy. I kept our bargain. I won't hurt you. I just want to hold you.'

Cathy tried to lie still and calm in his arms, but it was odd, feeling someone else there in the bed with her. She lay rigid for a while, but Dev was breathing slowly, regularly, and did not move. She felt her body relaxing, coming alive.

'Are you asleep, Dev?' she asked, tentatively.

'No.'

'Do you remember that night I was ill in Hamilton Square? You held my hand. It was okay.' She put her hand over his. It was tense, the fingers hard against her waist. She stroked it gently and after a moment the stiffness went, the fingers opened and curved about her hip.

'I know we haven't been getting along too well, but maybe when I get back...' He leaned over and kissed her lightly, gently, but now Cathy was trembling, wildly aroused by his nakedness, by the pressure of his body on her. She put her arms around his neck and clung to him.

'Cathy...?'

She touched him, her hands slipping down his body. He began kissing her again, differently, desperately. Cathy could feel him shaking, and responded helplessly. He pushed up her short nightdress, baring her breasts, pressing delicately with his fingertips.

Cathy gasped, 'Dev...'

'Why not? You let Chris, on the side stage tonight.'

Cathy's mind blanked, horrified. 'You don't think I...'

But Dev wasn't listening. He was caressing her body, his long hands moving over her, trembling, adoring, his fingers stoking, sliding in the smooth skin of her groin. 'I love you, Cathy. Please let me. You want me. Sweet little baby...'

Sweet little baby.

His voice was hoarse. He had said that the first night under the apple tree when he had taken her. It all came back agonisingly.

Cathy went rigid, panting, and tried to push his hands away.

'Sweet little baby,' he had said, and then forced into her, invading, his face like an evil silver mask, his hands bruising, blood from his broken lip in her mouth.

*Sweet little baby...*Blood wedding. A blood *baby?* The taste of blood filled her mouth and throat again, choking. She rolled over, frantically, thrusting away his hands and ran blindly for the bathroom.

Later, she was sick again, and towards dawn Dev turned away, lying on his back, not touching her now, staring at the ceiling.

'It's no good, is it? You haven't forgotten or forgiven anything. I know I did a bad thing, but does that mean I can't be sorry, that I can't ever be forgiven?'

'I don't know!' Cathy was close to hysteria. 'You know I don't do it on purpose. *I can't help it.*'

'I've tried to get near you, Cathy. I want to be warm and close, but when I reach out you slip away like a ghost.'

'You don't seem real to me either,' Cathy said. '*Nothing* seems real to me now. Except the concert tonight.'

She turned on her side away from him, tears sliding noiselessly down into her pillow. Knowing about the failure and defeat – that had been real enough.

Eventually she dropped into an exhausted sleep. In the morning Dev had gone, not bothering to wake her to say goodbye.

Chapter Nine

With Dev and Chris and their mad entourage gone, peace descended on Cox's Farm. Everybody relaxed. George Kaye sat in the kitchen in the morning chatting with the workmen, and Mrs. Kaye spent most of her time thinking up special recipes to tempt Cathy's appetite.

But Cathy hardly noticed. She was painting again. Working in a kind of delirium, an ecstasy, as the logjam of her creativity burst free. She spent all her time now in the barn, returning to the house only to fall into bed and sleep. It irritated her that her pregnancy made her need more rest and she could not go on painting into the night as she usually did. If only the baby would hurry up and come. She felt big and uncomfortable. But the ideas were pouring out faster than she could get them down. She needed every available minute.

She found that her painting had become simpler, more powerful and direct, and there was a new sombreness and tension underlying the paintings, a greater depth than there had been in her work before, a knowledge of pain and failure and the limits of being human.

She was working on the drawings she had made at the concert. Expanding, changing, refining. She made detailed drawings, studies analysing the light and dark, the refractive light, the movement. Some were so complex that they looked like abstract paintings. She made separate studies of the faces of the fans, of Dev and Chris moving in different positions, of the interplay of coloured lights, the flashing mirrors. But all the time she was working towards a special painting, one she could not yet envisage or define. She must bring together the lights, the patterns of movement and colour, but also the feeling of the concert, the excitement, the connection. There were the feelings of the fans – and the feelings of Chris and Dev, stalking and crouching and dangerous, and their magical apartness, the aura of great stars, trapped in bars of light.

There were her own feelings too. What the evening had meant to her. Her realisation that you had to take charge of your own life and could not blame others for your own weaknesses. It would all need to be included before she would be satisfied. It would be the most difficult and the most important painting she had ever made.

'Yes, what is it? *Hello*?' Cathy said, irritably.

'I'm sorry I haven't phoned before,' Dev's voice said, abruptly. 'We've been moving about so much and it's a crazy circus as usual. I didn't want to wake you in the middle of the night.'

'It's all right,' said Cathy, surprised. 'What do you want, Dev?'

The silence lengthened over the telephone line.

'*Want*?'

'Well, it must cost the earth to telephone from Japan – if that's where you are.'

'For chrissakes, I thought you might be upset, might be waiting for a call...'

'Well no,' said Cathy. 'I've been so busy I haven't had time. Was there something special?'

His voice was suddenly vicious. The line crackled with his anger. 'Listen, sweetheart, it's the custom, see? Husbands, *even* rock musicians, are expected to telephone their pregnant wives and show concern.'

'Oh I'm fine,' said Cathy, relieved. 'I feel great. There's no need to bother to ring. I know you're all tied up with the concerts. I've got a list of the numbers and places you gave me if there's anything.'

His voice was silky. 'Yeah, I noticed all your letters piled up waiting for me at the hotels. Three weeks without a phone call and I can hear how really worried you are about *me.*'

Cathy flushed. 'I'm sorry...I never thought...I mean, I know they'd get in touch with me if there was anything...How *is* the tour going?'

'Go to hell!' said Dev, and smashed the received down.

Cathy worked until the baby came. Occasionally she saw the village doctor, and sent Dev brief, dutiful letters reporting on the check-ups. But it was difficult to write to Dev. Every day was the same in Nethercombe.

To her surprise Chris wrote to her regularly, twice a week at least, sometimes more often, about the places they played, the gigs, the sightseeing, the people they met, hilarious stories about life on the road. Cathy enjoyed reading them and felt she had begun to know Chris much better.

But Dev did not write. Every few weeks when he received one of her letters, there would be a furious telephone call, which ended each time in a quarrel. He always sounded angry and impatient.

'Can't you write a letter longer than a page and a half?'

'There's nothing to say. You don't want to hear about my painting or the daffodils under the trees, do you?'

'Out of sight, out of mind, isn't it?' Dev said, bitterly.

'You're not out of my mind,' said Cathy, surprised, remembering the piled drawings and studies of the concert. She had thought about Dev and Chris more intensively than she had ever done before, trying to understand them, trying to understand the thing that set them apart from ordinary people. In a strange way she felt closer to Dev now than when he was physically present, pushing into her private space and having to be resisted. It seemed impossible that he was not aware of it.

She had spent an afternoon, sitting on the floor of the north-facing room, her arms clasped around her knees, looking again at his paintings, which she had propped around the walls. The reaching hand shape fascinated her, and what was the escaping blaze of light? Fire? Diamonds? She had gone away at last, feeling upset. Dev might act ruthless and strong, but his paintings said he was driven by a terrible insecurity, always losing what he most wanted.

In the garden room she found a whole shelf of books about Easy Connection. Pictorial biographies in English and German, souvenir programmes in a dozen languages. *Easy Connection-The Early Years*; *The Connection-The Rock Superstars in the States; The Connection-In their own Words.* She read them carefully, trying to understand.

They were all heavily censored as far as she could see. The scandals were played down. There were pictures of the wives of Leo and Keith, veiled references to an American heiress who had been Dev's 'girl friend', and even more veiled references to the bad times they had gone through as a result, only to emerge more brilliant than ever before. Whoever the girl was, Dev must have loved her very much, Cathy thought.

The early pictures showed them looking incredibly young and eager, larking about. What had happened to them over the years to turn them into these world-weary aristocrats of rock on the end pages, cynically watching the world, at once wary and dangerous? No wonder she could not seem to get through to Dev. His defences were rock hard.

The more she read the books, the more incredible it seemed that Dev had married her. She had absolutely nothing for a man who had been everywhere and done everything. Dev could not be serious about her. One day he would grow tired of his toy.

The days went past quickly, uncounted. The baby came three weeks early. Dev had made absurd and elaborate arrangements for a private nursing home and the famous gynaecologist to be on hand, but there was no time to use them. The baby was born suddenly, near dawn, at Cox's Farm, with Mrs. Kaye helping the village midwife, and later Dr. Eliot, his trousers pulled on over his pyjamas.

'Do you want to hold him?'

'No.'

The baby wailed thinly.

Mrs. Kaye covered-up quickly for her. 'I expect you're tired, Cathy, love. You need to sleep.'

'Nice it was so quick and easy,' said the midwife, sniffily.

Easy.

Cathy forced the words, slurred with exhaustion and pain. 'Is it all right? Is it normal?'

The midwife was shocked. 'He's gorgeous. A beautiful little boy. The prettiest baby this month so far.'

'Small and delicate, like a faery child,' Mrs. Kaye was smiling.

Cathy shivered. 'Not *marked*?'

'Of course not!' The midwife was cross. 'If you held him you could see.'

'I don't want to,' Cathy said, and turned her face into the pillow. Over at last. She dropped into blessed sleep.

When she woke, the sun was high. All the paraphernalia of the birth had been tidied away. You would never know about all the blood and the afterbirth and mess and slippery rubber sheets, Cathy thought. The room was rich and elegant, the morning sunlight streaming through the tall windows draped in heavy pink silk. Civilised. But there was nothing civilised about birth. It was real and primitive. Nothing to do with May flowers in pottery bowls and deep pile shell pink carpets. Dev would be disappointed. He had so much wanted to be there when the baby was born. He would feel she had cheated him again.

The baby was next to her bed, sleeping in the absurd, frilled muslin cot that Mary had chosen for her, along with all the other baby things.

Cathy stared down at him. Mrs. Kaye was right. He was beautiful, not creased and red like most babies. He was pale and exquisite, his head covered in fine gold hair. There was no sign of any of the hideous birth marks, a punishment for the way he had come into being, which Cathy had dreamed about night after night.

As she watched, the baby opened his eyes and tried to focus on her face. He began to cry loudly.

The midwife came quickly through the door. 'Oh good, you're awake, Mrs. Devlin. Baby wants his breakfast. Isn't he a sweetie? What are you going to call him?'

'I don't know,' said Cathy. 'Dev will say.'

The nurse looked at her curiously, as she picked up the baby and put him into Cathy's arms.

'But I don't want to feed him myself. I already told the doctor...' Cathy's voice rose.

'Now, now, you have to at first. It's the colostrum. It gives the baby protection against all kinds of diseases. Now come along, Mother.' Her voice was firm, allowing no argument. She was on familiar ground now. Millionaire rock star's wife or not, mothers must feed their babies.

Cathy took the baby awkwardly. 'All right,' she said, reluctantly. 'Just to begin with.'

'Hold his head. Poor baby's head is dropping.'

Cathy held the baby's head carefully and he began to suck contently. She hoped that it would make her feel like a proper mother. Countless paintings and movies of mothers suckling their babies with love, romantic and beautiful, came into her mind.

But then, they had been loving wives, she thought bitterly, and their babies were not the result of violence and rape.

She took a long breath and forced herself to look at the baby. His muscles and face were screwed into ecstasy as he lost her milky nipple and found it again. His hands moved fitfully, the tiny fingers opening and stretching in delight. The nails were perfect miniatures. She touched the delicate gold hair with the tips of her fingers. Impossible to believe he was the result of violence and ugliness. The thought came to her then that he might have come from the loving afterwards.

Mrs. Kaye had telephoned Dev with the news of the baby's early arrival, and reported that he was shaken and wildly excited. He had kept her on the telephone for nearly an hour, demanding all the details. He said that after the next concert he was going to fly home.

Cathy groaned. She wanted to be alone for a while to get used to the baby and sort out her feelings. She knew that Dev would be like a hawk, critically watching her every move, noting every emotion.

Later in the day he telephoned again. 'Are you okay?'

'Yes, I'm fine,' Cathy said. 'Mrs. Kaye told you.'

'Was it bad? Did it hurt?'

'Yes, it hurt. They said it was quick. But it seemed a long time.'

Dev said, after a moment. 'I wanted to be there.'

'I know. I'm sorry you're disappointed. I didn't do it on purpose. The baby was in a hurry!' She hesitated, took a deep breath, and said, shyly, 'I'm sorry you weren't there with me, Dev. I wanted you.'

He said, abruptly, 'Cathy, they've added another three dates in the States without telling me. Another week.'

Suddenly, perversely, Cathy was so upset she felt like crying.

'It's all right. It's not long.'

'Cathy, I want to see you so much. I could fly back for a few hours if you think...'

'I said, it's all right,' she said, sharply. 'The baby is fine too. Fair, tiny, healthy, *normal.* He's not disfigured and deformed. You don't have to worry.'

'*Deformed*? Are you crazy?'

'Well, I thought he might be...marked...or something. Th-the way it happened.'

There was a long silence.

'Yeah, well you got the dirty thing out of your body at last, Cathy,' he said, quoting her.

Cathy flinched, and took a shaky breath. She did not want to remember all the arguments, all the bitter words they had used like knives to slash each other. It seemed as though it had all happened in another life, in those dark months of worry and fear. She felt quite differently now.

'Cathy, are you there? Cathy? I'm sorry. I shouldn't have dragged that up. How do you feel about him?'

'I don't know,' said Cathy. 'He's...beautiful. What are you going to call him, Dev? He has to be registered.'

'What am *I* calling him? What are you trying to do, Cathy, pretend he's nothing to do with you?'

Very carefully, Cathy put the telephone down and sat, white and hunched up. For a moment she had thought there was a chance to change things, but they were quarrelling as badly as ever.

The highly qualified nurse Dev had hired, arrived, smiling and super-efficient. Cathy was relieved. Sue Bloom was in her early twenties. She was an Easy Connection fan, thrilled to be working for Paul Devlin. Did Chris Carter, her all-time rave and heart-throb ever come to the Farm?

Cathy smiled, grimly, 'He practically lives here.'

'Oh, fantastic! Will he talk to me?'

Cathy looked at her plump prettiness, and wondered how long it would take Chris.

'He's not...standoffish,' she said, and laughed aloud.

Sue flushed. 'Oh, I'm sorry. I shouldn't be talking like that, Mrs. Devlin, but I'm so excited at being here, and the baby is such a little love!' She picked him up and cuddled him, swinging round the room. The baby made glugging noises but did not seem to mind.

For a week they all hung over the new baby – Cathy, the Kayes, the cleaners, even the studio builders – making stupid noises to amuse him, and tickling his toes, until Sue Bloom eventually chased them away, making it plain that she wanted to get on with her job without too much interference.

Reluctantly Cathy went back to the difficult painting waiting on her easel. But she knew that Sue Bloom was trustworthy and caring, and as soon as she started painting seriously again it drew her like a magnet and she spent longer and longer in the barn.

She knew now that the special painting she was working towards would be a joint portrait of Dev and Chris, life-size, in the smoky silver beams, but it was giving her so much trouble she could not believe she would ever get it exactly right. She had done more studies, full-length paintings even but still the exact feeling eluded her.

In between times she made a special effort to do her post-natal exercises. She swam in the pool daily and her body recovered quickly. It was marvellous to be free of the heavy lumpishness. She began to feel really well for the first time in months.

The heaviness began to lift from her mind too. The veil of dark nightmare had been drawn back somehow. She had found her way back to her painting, and the baby was healthy and whole. She had thought of it for a long time as something dirty and alien, occupying her body without her consent. It seemed now that a large part of her sickness and physical revulsion might have come from her fear and guilt that the baby had been harmed in some way.

There was another change too. Since she had looked at the early pictures of Easy Connection she had begun to feel differently about Dev. She did not feel sick now at the thought of lying in his arms. Perhaps, when he came she could explain, and they could overcome the quarrels and tensions and they could start a real married life.

Dev surely wouldn't be willing to wait any longer. The night before he had gone away had made that plain. Cathy felt apprehensive, but excited too. Her pulses beat faster, remembering the feel of his body against her own. She was sure it would be all right now.

The weather grew very warm and Sue put the baby on blankets and cushions on the sunny terrace overlooking the pool, free to kick and stretch.

Cathy found them there one afternoon as she came from the barn. Sue Bloom was looking after him beautifully, very loving and competent. There was very little for Cathy to do, except play with him.

She sat down and took the baby on her lap. He clutched her finger with the marvellously miniature hands and tiny nails and seemed to know her. He yawned, opening his clear grey eyes and suddenly, for a fraction of a second he looked so like Dev that she nearly dropped him. She stared at him, but the likeness had gone. The baby, disliking her intense gaze, began to cry. She put him back into his cushions, smiled absently at Sue, and walked back to the studio. There was the familiar excitement rising and shaking her hands, keeping her moving restlessly, unable to settle.

The next day she brought a sketch block and pencil with her to the terrace and began a new series of meditation drawings, staring for hours at the baby and then drawing with swift, flowing economical lines. But the pencil line was too thin to catch the rounded softness and she turned to pastels and began her famous series of baby drawings. The baby got used to her grave stare and forgot her, finding he could move his hands, his feet, crowing with love and joy in being alive.

The deep observation made Cathy aware of the minute advances in the baby's progress, the increasing control, the fantastic growth rate. Nothing was ever the same twice. The drawings were not sentimental. They showed the baby's intense efforts to understand, to *grow*. And they brought Cathy very close to him. She began to feel a personal interest and involvement. She looked forward each day to seeing what new things the baby had achieved. And she looked forward now to Dev coming home, wanting to show him the drawings and talk to him about the baby.

Chapter Ten

But when at last Dev came home everything was different.

Cathy went to meet him, but the car was late, caught up in traffic and when she arrived she could not get through the huge crowd of fans crushed against the security barrier. She stood in the crowd, shaking, surprised at how excited she felt at seeing him again.

The Easy Connection road crew started to come through the gate with trolleys loaded with luggage and instruments. Bill Hopkins appeared with Leo Field, Keith Hurst and his wife, and then Dev and Chris together.

Dev's eyes were glittering and weary. His long hands flicked a casual, practised greeting to the fans and shouting photographers. Cool, beautiful, magnetic. Everybody's idea of the successful rock idol. Her husband. A total stranger. Cathy felt chilled and shy.

Chris, wearing a wide-brimmed leather hat, grinned and waved to the crowd, which surged forward, and Cathy saw then that there was a girl between Dev and Chris, her arms linked in theirs. She was flushed, laughing up at them. Her white linen shorts moulded themselves to her body without a crease. She had Gucci boots and a cream silk shirt hung with chunky gold chains. She had a big leather satchel and a leather hat to match Chris', hanging round her neck like a cowgirl. For a moment Cathy thought she knew her, but in seconds they had all swept past her into the press lounge, not seeing her – *not looking for her.*

Cathy fought her way out of the crowd and walked back to the car slowly.

Dev came home hours later, bringing Chris and a rowdy group of the road crew. They came in three cars, skidding to a halt in front of the house and erupting, yelling and laughing into the entrance hall. They all seemed to be in that state of wild elation which Cathy could recognise now as the result of exhaustion, excitement and too much to drink.

She smiled, covering her disappointment, wishing they would all go away quickly, so that she could tell Dev...Tell Dev *what?* What could she say to this cold, glittering, sophisticated stranger?

Chris grabbed her and hugged and kissed her deeply, before disappearing upstairs for a shower. Dev gave her a quick peck on the cheek, not touching her, as though he had just come back from an hour's trip, she thought, indignantly.

'Hello, Cathy. You look different.' His eyes, narrowing and darkening, took in her paint stained jeans and shirt, the glowing tanned skin, the golden tendrils escaping from her tied-up hair.

She smiled at him. 'Better, I hope. Goodbye ghost.'

'Yeah,' he looked her over, mocking. 'Our tour seems to have been good for you.'

Which is more than she could say for *him*, she thought. He looked gaunt and tired, his eyes red-rimmed and bloodshot.

'You've got paint on your nose.' He sounded disapproving, angry. She pushed the thought away.

'Sorry,' she rubbed it off and grinned happily at him. 'Oh Dev, I am glad to see you. Come and look at the baby.'

'Where is he?'

'In bed.'

'I'll look in later.' His voice was casual, empty.

'*Later?* I thought you would want to...'

'Not now. I want a drink.'

She stared at him, remembering his obsessive desire for this child. What was the matter with him? He was so cold and remote. It was all going wrong. She turned, blinking away tears and saw Chris coming down the stairs, grinning at her.

'Incredible! Fair hair. Grey eyes. He looks just like me!'

Everybody laughed. Cathy went bright red. 'He looks like all three of us!' she said, angrily.

Later, when she went in to the baby, Dev was there, staring down at the sleeping child.

She said, 'So you came after all.'

'He's smaller than I thought'

'I thought you weren't interested.'

'I'm interested...Are *you?*'

She did not look at him and did not see the appeal in his eyes.

'You took your time.'

'I wanted to do it properly – with you – not with all the crowd.'

'Chris came straight away.'

The light went out in his eyes. 'How was it? I was ready to fly home, but we had the big concert in Chicago, and Chris thought it would be better to wait.'

'You told me,' Cathy said. 'It doesn't matter.'

Dev said, curiously, 'George Kaye said you came to meet us. Why'd you chicken out, Cathy? What happened to you?'

She shrugged. 'I couldn't get through the crowd or past the security men.'

'You only had to tell them you were my wife!'

'I did. The man said that he was Frank Sinatra and just stay where I was or I'd get hurt.'

Dev was angry. 'That's ridiculous. You should have...'

Cathy shrugged again. 'It was a stupid idea anyway. I saw you all walk out and I realised I wouldn't fit in. You were all so exciting, glamorous...'

'What the hell are you talking about? I never guessed you'd come to meet us.'

She said, with an effort, 'Who was the girl, Dev? There was a girl with you. Very rich. Like a film star.'

'Charis? You've met her. She was here the day we met.'

Charis. Spectacularly sexy in a disco outfit, but with her eyes blank like a dead person, deep in a drug trip on the sofa. A cold feeling moved down Cathy's spine. 'I didn't recognise her. She looked so different. Alive.'

He gave an odd laugh. 'Yeah, she burns, man. Her father owns half the arms factories in the States. She's not always stoned.' He laughed again.

'She came to meet you?'

He looked at her for a moment, sharply, and then away. He said, too casually, 'She was along for part of the trip.'

Cathy felt a surge of resentment, and a deeper feeling she did not want to recognise. Jealousy. Fear.

'With Chris – or you?'

'She likes travelling with the band.' He sounded amused.

Cathy stared out of the window into the warm dusk. She watched Chris and Sue Bloom walking towards the water meadow. He was holding her hand.

'I missed you, Cathy. Did you miss me?' Dev said, softly, behind her, and put his hands on her shoulders. She shrugged them away resentfully.

'You could have come with us. I asked you.'

She moved away from him, still unreasonably angry. 'There were other things I had to do.'

'The baby is beautiful, Cathy. I never thought...'

'And I've started to paint again. Dev, I'm so pleased...'

The baby woke up suddenly, smiling as usual, and Dev picked him up delighted. 'We'll have to find a smashing name for you, my son,' he said looking him in the eye gravely.

The baby, excited, smacked him across the nose with his tiny waving fist. Dev laughed. 'So you're taking after your old man already. What about Henry, or Joe, or Mohammed...'

'He's already got a name.'

Dev stared at her, his eyes kindling and laid the baby back carefully in his cot. 'Listen, Cathy, I've got news for you. When a man and a woman have a baby together, they discuss certain important things, like his name, how he's going to be brought up. It's a joint responsibility.'

'I *asked* you what you wanted to call him.'

'I said *discuss.*'

Cathy shrugged, irritated. 'I told you, he had to be registered.'

'Well? Don't you think I've got a right to know what you've called him?'

'Paul, Christopher, Howard.'

He paused, trying to read her expression. 'You called him after me?'

'Who else? You, your friend and your father. You are his father. There's no argument about that.'

He understood suddenly. 'Nothing to do with *you,* Cathy? Nothing for your family?'

'You think I want to be reminded of my *father*? My *brother*?'

He watched her coldly. 'What about Nick? Or – what did Chris suggest? – Tom? Dave? You see anything of Tom Gibbon or Dave Hampton while we've been away?'

'Of course not!' Cathy drew a shaky breath. She *must* make it right. *Now.* Before it got any worse. She made an enormous effort, her heart banging heavily. 'Dev, there's something I've got to say.' She stared at the carpet, the colour burning her cheeks. 'Since the baby came I...Well, I mean, I feel...'

Dev interrupted, wearily. 'Cathy, I'm dead beat. Do we have to talk about it now? Can't it wait till the morning?'

Relief. Despair. 'Please, it's very important.'

'I know. We'll talk later.'

But there was no talk later. Dev went away with Bill Hopkins to an urgent business meeting instead.

Chris, stretched out on one of the sofas in the garden room, with a plate of pâté from the cold buffet by the door, said accusingly, 'You never answered any of my letters, Cathy.'

She flushed guiltily. 'I'm sorry. I didn't know what to write. Nothing happens here.'

Chris laughed, disbelievingly. 'You didn't write, Cathy, because you don't give a damn.'

'I enjoyed reading your letters, Chris.'

'Have you any idea what it's like being away for months and not knowing what's happening to the people you love? Even my mother took time off from the chihuahuas and wrote a few lines.'

Cathy said, sarcastically, 'You're not trying to tell me that you've been lonely for me? You told me about the traditional comforts of a touring band – booze, dope, girls.'

Chris looked at her, and then away. 'Dev's married now.'

Cathy said, carefully, 'There were girls?'

'There are always girls.'

'Come on, Chris, you know what I mean. You've been gone three months.'

Chris hesitated. 'Yeah, well, there were girls. Dev was a bit turned on. What can you expect in the circumstances? But honestly, it doesn't mean a thing.'

'It doesn't?' Suddenly it seemed obvious why he had been so cold and remote.

'The things you do on the road – they're not real.'

So Dev was over his infatuation with her and was playing the field again. So what? She had always known it would happen, hadn't she?

'Cathy, you're not upset?'

She turned away to the open french windows, not
wanting Chris to see. 'I didn't think it would happen so
quickly.'

Chris said, softly, 'You don't ask about me.'

She smiled, reluctantly. 'I already know! But please
leave Sue Bloom alone. She's for the baby. I don't want her
leaving.'

He grinned. 'I promise I won't sleep around when we're
married, Cathy. I won't need to, will I?'

She stepped out on to the terrace and let the curtain fall
behind her, glad of the cool night air on her hot cheeks.

The next morning, after a disturbed night, Cathy screwed
up her courage to speak to Dev again, shaking with shyness
and embarrassment. It was a bad time. Dev was impatient
and in a hurry, on his way up to town again. He had a day
of press interviews to get through, one every half-hour, he
said. He looked exhausted already, as though he had not
slept.

'But you've only just got back,' Cathy said.

Dev shrugged. 'Everyone wants to know about the tour.'
He sat down next to her. 'Okay, Cathy, what do you want to
talk about? As if I didn't know.'

'You *know?*' she said, confused. 'Dev, this isn't the right
time, here in the entrance hall. I'll tell you when you come
back. When you're not in a hurry.'

'Come on, Cathy. Get it over with. I haven't got time to
play games. Christ, I feel tired.' He stretched out his legs
and leaned his head back on the sofa, his eyes closed. 'I
wish I could stay here all day.'

Cathy watched his face, the skin drawn tautly across the
high cheek bones. His eyelashes were thick and dark. 'You
ought to take some time off. Can't Chris do some of the
interviews?'

He smiled. 'When he gets bored he gets rude and starts telling the truth. The last time we had two slander suits and a BBC ban on our record. He *explained* it. Line by line. In Anglo-Saxon. For a guy who takes the *Tao of Physics* on tour as light reading, Chris can get pretty basic.'

Cathy laughed. 'Nothing he did would ever surprise me.'

Dev opened his eyes, the dark grey intense. 'Why didn't you write a proper letter to me, Cathy? All those duty letters.'

'I didn't know what to write. We had so many quarrels.'

He closed his eyes again, and she saw that his hands were curled into fists, the knuckles shining white. 'Say what you've got to say.'

She stared down at him, trying to find the words. But suddenly, there were no words. Only the nearness of his full mouth and the warmth of his body. She put out her hand and touched the dark shadows under his eyes with the tips of her fingers, and then, unable to stop herself, she bent her head and kissed his mouth, softly, like a butterfly. Dev did not move. She kissed him again.

'Dev?'

The silence stretched and then Chris came leaping down the stairs shouting for Gregg.

'There's a photo session, Dev. I'll come up to town with you.'

'Okay.'

Cathy got up quickly and moved away. 'Have a good day both of you.'

Chris came back the following afternoon, and threw himself on the old divan in the barn, folding his arms behind his head, sighing with pleasure. 'Thank God to be home.'

'Where's Dev?' Cathy heard the stiffness in her voice.

Chris raised an eyebrow. 'Wifely concern and interest, Cathy? That's not like you. Turning over a new leaf?'

Cathy flushed. 'I wanted to talk to him.'

'He's busy.'

'I want to know when he'll be back, Chris.'

'Let's just say he's not likely to be hurrying back at the moment.'

'Oh?' Cathy turned her back, and started to mix some paint on her palette.

'Tara Linstrom is in town. Model of the Year. An old flame.'

Her fingers tightened on the brush. She felt ill, remembering the way she had kissed him. He must have laughed himself silly with Chris.

'I'm not proud,' said Chris. 'I'll take the crumbs from the rich man's table.'

Cathy looked at him, confused.

'You got any kisses like yesterday going spare, I could use them.'

It was only then that Cathy realised that Chris must have seen her kissing Dev. Had he interrupted deliberately?

She said, her heart beating rapidly, ignoring the surge of sensuality his voice roused. 'There's not enough to go round.'

Chris laughed softly. 'There's more than enough, Cathy. You just don't know how much yet. A feast for the gods.' His eyes moved slowly over her breasts and down her body. 'Milk and honey.'

By the time Dev came back, a week later, muttering about studio business, Cathy had admitted to herself the stupidity of believing anything could be done to rescue the marriage.

The summer was hot and fine. Dev lounged by the pool, swimming and sunbathing with Chris and Sue Bloom, playing with baby Paul. Already the baby recognised and adored him, chuckling with pleasure and excitement when he came.

Dev did not ask about her work. He never came to the barn now, and she put the baby drawings away. She could not concentrate on drawing the baby, with Chris and Dev there, watching her sardonically.

There was a hard shell of indifference about Dev. He was very cool and distant. In fact, he hardly spoke to her at all. Sometimes he seemed almost to be waiting for something. Cathy wondered if he was trying to find a way to tell her that it was all finished between them. He needn't worry, she thought proudly, I won't pester him. He won't have trouble getting rid of me if that's what he wants.

Nothing was said of the holiday in Hawaii, and nothing more was said of her joining the Easy Connection tour to the States in the late autumn.

Cathy did not know how she could get closer to Dev, unsure even if it was a good idea to try. She retreated to the barn and plunged gratefully back into her work.

In June, Caleb Crow showed her early figure drawings and gouache studies in his Mixed Summer Exhibition. All the drawings were sold, and she had three portrait commissions. Harrison Lane, the most influential of the art critics, devoted most of his weekly review to her work.

Cathy was very pleased, but already she was working for her one-woman show in October, which was what really counted. She knew that few young artists were fortunate in getting a Caleb Crow exhibition at the Arundell in the first year of their contract. She wanted only her very best work on show.

In particular she wanted to complete the difficult painting of Chris and Dev at Wembley. It had evolved into two canvases, each three metres high and two metres wide, cleated together to form one big painting. The background was a shifting kaleidoscope of blur and detail, silvery beams of light crossing and criss-crossing, smoke, cables, reflections on guitars and drums, very intricate.

The portrait of Dev was probably the best thing she had ever done, painted from sketches and memory when he was thousands of miles away. Dev, on stage, mobile, prowling, tiger-like, his guitar held casually, his face tense, his eyes dark and hypnotic, utterly alive.

It was the portrait of Chris, which was still giving her trouble. Chris was to be bending forward, arms out, laughing, his head back, but she could not, somehow, get the feeling right.

'You want more drawings? I'll model for you, if you like.' Chris was always poking about the barn, looking through her work, and he was fascinated by the big Wembley painting.

'I'm not sure.'

He said, grinning, 'You want me to take my clothes off? I'll take my clothes off for you any time, Cathy.'

'There isn't much to take off,' said Cathy, unamused. She did not want to admit, even to herself, that she found Chris, naked except for the tiny bikini brief, lounging brown and sensuous on the old divan in the shadows of the barn, deeply disturbing.

'What's the problem? What's holding it up?'

Cathy stared at the painting. 'I don't know. Maybe I do need more drawings. I just don't understand you, Chris. You're so many different people. Changing all the time. At the concert – you were frightening. I don't know what makes you tick.'

'I'll help you find out.'

She turned her back. 'No thanks. *I'm trying to work.*'

He laughed, very close, and kissed the nape of her neck. His lips were warm and soft.

'You are coming to our Welcome Back concert at Hammersmith tonight, aren't you, Cathy?'

'I wouldn't miss it,' Cathy said, trying to sound light. 'Maybe it'll give me another clue.' She moved away from him quickly, her body electric with response.

The concert was brilliant. Chris brought the house down singing, as an encore, an hilarious version of Diamond Joe Symmons' *Little Red Riding Hood*.

Little Red Riding Hood,
You're looking good.
Everything a beeeeeg, baaaaaad, WOLF, could want!

Chris was the prowling, rampant wolf, parading round Dev too closely, sniffing at him in unmentionable places, and Dev was a coy Little Red Riding Hood, playing his guitar above his head, writhing, apparently in an excess of sexual frenzy. The audience howled.

Cathy was not surprised, when she went backstage, using her passes, to find Bill Hopkins hopping mad.

He was standing in the middle of the crowded dressing room, waving his arms and shouting angrily, 'I tell you, you can't keep it in the act. You'll have the bloody press down on us again.'

All the band was there, swigging down cans of lager, their shirts and bodies glistening with sweat, their hair soaked as though they had been swimming.

Leo Field was bent over, convulsed with laughter; Keith Hurst, dark and saturnine, was sprawled on a bench grinning, and Dev and Chris, flushed and wound up, were holding on to each other, laughing hysterically.

'Do you hear me, Chris? I don't care how much it turned them on. Effing obscene it was! You want to stir up all that bi-sexual muck again?'

'Now come on, Bill old son, you're over-reacting,' said Pete Starr, the temporary second drummer, soothingly, trying to stop laughing. 'Come and have a wee dram and forget your troubles.' He drew him over to a table where someone was splashing whisky into glasses, winking at Dev over Bill's shoulder.

'*Over*-reacting?' Bill said, angrily. 'You trying managing this lot. There's no such thing as *over*-reacting.'

Chris, still laughing, dropped on to a chair, and stretched out his legs. Dev turned and handed him an opened beer can. Cathy, unnoticed, saw their hands touch, and Dev smiled down at Chris through half-closed eyes, a private, secret grin, meant for Chris alone. Chris looked back at him equivocally, his eyes full of suppressed laughter. There was an aura of almost visible sexual energy about them.

Friends. Closer than brothers, Chris had said. Cathy caught her breath. It simply couldn't be true – there had been so many girls! And yet...She tried to dismiss the idea, but it would not go away. 'You don't understand even now, do you Cathy? Don't want to understand,' Chris had said. She lay awake late, remembering that secret smile.

'How was it – our show, Cathy?' Chris said, next morning as they ate a late breakfast together, after Dev had left for town.

'Brilliant,' Cathy said, truthfully. 'You know you were great. You were all incredible.'

'Sexy?'

'Okay, very sexy.'

He smiled at her. 'We got a lot of stick last night. New business.'

'I heard. Bill said obscene. The newspaper says 'sexually ambiguous'.'

'We're still trying to figure it out. D'you reckon there's a tribe somewhere who rub bums, instead of noses like the Eskimoes?'

'It was the *Little Red Riding Hood* routine.'

Chris laughed. 'Yeah. Right. We're good at that kind of thing. Very inventive.'

Cathy was silent, not looking at him. She pushed the salt cellar around with her forefinger. 'Chris...you and Dev...'

His light eyes watched her mockingly. 'What about me and Dev?

'I know you've been friends for ever, but are you...I mean...' Blushing furiously she stumbled to a halt, realising the impossibility of asking him directly.

There was a brief silence, and then Chris said, casually, 'I love him. Is that what you want to know?'

'What does that mean?'

'Whatever you think it means, Cathy.'

'A-and Dev?'

'Why don't you ask him?'

He smiled lazily, watching her. 'Too long on the road, Cathy.'

'I don't understand.'

'Bobby Bare's song *I've got to Get Rid of This Band.* Too long on the road and one guy smells, one's too handsome, one drugs and two hold hands.'

She took a deep breath. 'Are you telling me you and Dev hold hands?'

His eyes were suddenly wide-open, laughing, right into her heart and mind. He was devastating. She felt breathless, trembling.

'Just remember, love, a triangle has got three sides.'

Cathy went out, slamming the door hard.

Chapter Eleven

Cathy was upset, forced to recognise for the first time how jealous she felt. If she didn't care for Dev or Chris why was she so jealous?

She buried herself in her work, shutting out the problems, so that even when present, she was abstracted, picking at her food, getting up in the middle of sentences and walking off, scarcely conscious that anyone was there. Chris watched her narrowly, biding his time.

Dev was away in town most days. He was supposed to be looking at the latest electronic recording equipment for the newly-built studio, seeing the engineers and technicians who would set it up.

Cathy hardly noticed that he was away, and did not realise that he was staying more and more often at his London flat until Chris suggested that she should find out who was staying there with him.

'*Staying* with him?' Cathy put her brushes down, and turned quickly. 'But he's working, isn't he? There's all that equipment. And then there's this album he's producing for Dave Hampton and Ronnie Craig, mixing the...'

Chris was smiling nastily. She coloured. 'You mean he's taking girls there?'

'Not girl*s*. A special lady.'

'How special? Who?'

'You ought to read your newspaper more often, Cathy. You must be the only one who doesn't know. Intimate little dinner parties...'

'Oh, *go away,* Chris! I'm trying to work!'

But when he had gone, she gave in to her gnawing jealousy and went over to the garden room to look through old copies of the *Mirror* and *Sun*.

There were newspaper pictures of Dev and Tara Linstrom kissing goodbye at Heathrow, where Tara was flying out on assignment. And there were newspaper pictures of Dev and Charis, stunning in a narrow white evening gown, at a charity concert, shopping in the West End, walking through Covent Garden.

It was only a matter of time before the marriage broke up, Cathy thought numbly, staring at the pictures. Dev had drifted so far away. She waited for him to tell her it was all over and ask for a divorce.

Instead, to her surprise, Dev asked her to go to a reception with him. Her heart leaped, and then she realised, just in time, that it must be an official function where wives were expected to appear.

'We're getting an award. Annual awards of the record industry. Do you mind coming along?'

'Of course I don't. I'm not pregnant now.'

'I didn't want to interrupt your work.'

Cathy thought he was being sarcastic, but he looked back at her seriously. She was astonished to see that he was uncertain, almost tentative. She felt herself softening, smiling at him shyly. 'I'd like to go with you.'

He smiled back, his eyes dark. 'It'd be nice having you with me again, Cathy.'

Chris said, loudly, 'Janey Adams, your favourite female singer will be there too. And Dave Hampton, of course. Did you know that Dave and Janey Adams have split up, Cathy? He didn't tell you when he was here last week?'

'He didn't say anything,' Cathy said, upset.

Dev said, sharply, 'He was here?'

'He's here a lot lately.' Chris laughed and looked at Cathy. 'He likes the scenery.'

'But why didn't he tell me?' said Cathy.

'He's not talking about it. She's married Jay Bird of the Bird Lovers on the rebound.'

'Oh no!' Cathy had tears in her eyes. 'Dave's so nice. I really hoped it would be all right for him.'

'We're all nice,' said Dev, bitterly. 'Why should it be any different for *him*?'

Janey Adams arrived at the reception in her black limousine, alone and late. Her manager was waiting for her at the hotel entrance, fiddling with his outdated Zapata moustache, looking worried. She could guess why.

'Janey, you ought to know, er, Dave Hampton's here.'

'Yes,' she said, expressionlessly, and went on pushing though the crowd.

'I thought you'd want to know.'

She relented. 'I guessed he'd be here. I can't avoid him for ever.'

But the pain when she saw him was greater than she imagined. He was talking with Paul Devlin and Chris Carter of Easy Connection and a girl, very beautiful, slender, her hair a pale, gleaming gold. Dave was laughing down at her. Janey's heart twisted. Then Dev put his arm, carefully casual, but possessive, on the girl's shoulder and she remembered where she had seen her. In the newspaper. Dev's wife. One of the Easy Connection scandals. The relief made her smile foolishly.

As though conscious of being watched, the girl looked up and stared back at her gravely. Her eyes were wide, very intense, as though they were seeing beyond the outer surface into the guarded secrets beneath. Uncanny. Janey shivered. Then the girl began to smile delightedly. Janey smiled back, briefly, recognising a fan and turned away.

She took a glass of wine, and then another. The great need was to forget Dave and stop worrying about Jay for a while. She shook hands, chatted, circulated around the room avoiding the place where she had last seen Dave, smiling to cue, wondering if she would ever get used to these kind of functions.

She was presented with her award for best singer and saw Paul Devlin accepting the best album award for the Connection, and then Dave was standing next to her, accepting the award for the best song. She tried not to look at him.

Mr. Baldwin, the boss of her record company, smiling suavely, was saying how much pleasure it would give them all if she would consent to sing for them. She could hardly refuse, she thought grimly, not even when she found Dave was playing the piano for her.

To Cathy's surprise, Janey did not sing any of the songs, which had been big hits for her. She sang the blues. The strong, golden voice, deepened and roughened by pain and experience, clutched at the heart.

The first songs were light, and people laughed. *My Very Good Friend, the Milkman* and *He was a Good Man as Good Men Go,* but now a complete silence had fallen on the room. Janey Adams was singing *St. James Infirmary.*

Cathy thought it said everything about the futility and the blighted hopes of her life. It was a hymn to all poor, overworked, unappreciated musicians who would never get an award, who couldn't stand the stress and the pressures, who had died of drug overdose in a cold, unglamorous world. She saw the impact on the famous faces around her. The song reminded them of the price others had paid for their own success. The casualties by the wayside.

She would never in all her life forget this moment. The transfixed room, as the harsh reality poured around them. Dev's face, empty, boney like a skeleton, his eyes bleak. She wondered how many of the people here had friends who had died too soon, their bright promise crumbling under heroin addiction.

The song ended and they paid Janey the finest
compliment of all. There was complete silence. She looked
at them and blushed deeply. Someone put a drink into her
hands. She stared at it for a moment and then held the clear
liquid up to the light.

'Absent friends!' she said and drank it straight down, and
then they were all clapping wildly.

'She's *crying*,' Cathy said, shaken, to Chris next to her.

'Jay Bird was busted last week. He's been in the special
ward since.'

'A breakdown?'

'*Smack.*'

Startled, Cathy looked at Janey, and at Dave who was
sitting quite still looking at the keyboard. How could she
bear to sing about it? No, Janey was an artist, she would
have to sing about it.

There was a stir by the door, and people started to turn
round. Through the crowd, came a tall young man, very
striking in a room full of striking people. He was painfully
thin, with silver-gilt hair and blazing green eyes, dressed
from head to foot in sombre black leather.

'For God's sake, will you look at that,' said Dev,
beginning to laugh. 'I always thought she was a witch. She's
conjured him up.'

'It's Jay Bird?'

His face was narrow and dead white, except for the
brilliant eyes. He looked wild and reckless and Cathy
wondered why Janey, who surely could have had any man
she wanted, had married him. He looked as though he
would be an even more uncomfortable husband than Dev.
He stood, poised lightly, his gaze travelling swiftly around
the room until he saw Janey. Then he was across the room,
his arms round her and kissing her fiercely. People crowded
round, laughing and patting his back.

'Are you all right?' Janey was half-laughing, half-crying, hugging him. 'Why didn't you phone? Why did you come here?'

Cathy saw the wild laughter in his eyes and knew why Janey had married him.

'I had to. Where is he? Do you think I don't read the awards?'

'Looking for me, Jay?' Dave got up from the keyboard. 'Janey's in the middle of a set.'

'I've finished.'

'No you haven't,' said Jay, 'Sing *In the Heat of the Night* for me, Janey.' He was looking at Dave.

'Sing it for both of us, Janey!' said Dave, and walked away. Startled, Cathy saw Janey's eyes as they followed him.

Some of the people began to clap, someone else sat down at the piano, and Janey began to sing the old Ray Charles number, and again, an uncanny hush descended. Her voice was like thick cream, heavy with sensuousness.

Cathy thought she had never heard anything so sexy in her life. How could one voice express so much? She swallowed and found she was not breathing easily. She glanced sideways at Chris and found he was looking at her, his light eyes shining silver. Helplessly her eyes locked with his, and a slow deep blush burned up her neck and cheeks to her forehead and glowed hotly. She hid her hands in the folds of her skirt, but she knew that Chris had seen them shaking.

'I want to paint her,' Cathy said, trancelike, on the way home in the car. 'I've *got* to paint her.'

'Our baby's got a crush on Janey Adams!' Chris said, laughing.

Cathy said seriously, 'I think she's fantastic. The way she was tonight. The way she turns her head and moves her hands. The way her hair swings. And her voice is incredible. It sends a shiver over me.'

'I'll ask her,' said Dev.

'You *know* her?'

'Since she was sixteen.'

Something in his voice made her look at him. She said, hostile, 'I suppose you've been with her.'

Dev laughed across at Chris. 'We tried,' he admitted. 'But Janey Adams doesn't go in for screwing around, even if it's steam heat every time she sings. Even Chris couldn't make her.'

Chris laughed. 'Remember her in that little towel, Dev, at that festival someplace?'

'Hastings.'

'Yeah, right. Wowee!'

'*Towel?*' Cathy was incredulous, thinking of Janey Adams, dramatic and intense, burning like magnesium, as she sang the blues.

'Do you think she would sit for me?' she said. 'Dave was going to ask her, but maybe he forgot. I know just how I want to paint her.'

But it turned out that Janey Adams had a packed schedule of concerts and personal appearances all over the country. There was no time available for sittings. But she was excited about the idea of having her portrait painted, and promised to make some time when she came back from her Northern tour in the autumn.

The faces at the party haunted Cathy. Their laughter. Their reckless living, their desperation, their style. The price they paid.

'There's always a price,' Caleb had said. 'Music. Painting. There's always a price.'

The next day she started to make studies for the series of life-size portraits of rock musicians, which made her famous. She did not understand why, but she felt she must begin, urgently, with the drawings of Jay Bird.

Chapter Twelve

Dev was hardly ever at home now. When he was there, Cathy saw only the cool, glittering rock star, a stranger who swept through the house occasionally and disappeared again, without bothering to explain what he was doing, where he was going, or when he would be back, always surrounded by frantic, noisy people demanding his attention.

Dev was busy, but Chris was at the Farm all the time. Cathy did more drawings of him for the big portrait. He spent the days sprawled by the pool with his stereo, reading, or lounging on her divan watching her paint, waiting.

'Haven't you got anything else to do?' she said, irritably.

He smiled. 'Not until the new studio is ready. I'm not a workaholic like Dev. What's the matter, I'm bothering you?'

'No!' But it wasn't true.

Chris was deeply tanned, his hair bleached lighter by the sun, male, lazily seductive. She was conscious of him all the time now; the sexual tension was tight between them. She knew he was deliberately winding it tighter, but was too inexperienced to know how to stop him.

He smiled at her provocatively. 'You're lying, Cathy. I'm bothering you a lot.' He stretched and wandered over to look at her painting. He was too close. Cathy jerked away, and he laughed aloud.

'Fire burn...crackle, crackle,' he said, and still laughing, walked out to the pool. Soon, through the open door, she heard the sound of Elmore James, *It Hurts Me Too,* loud from the stereo.

The temperature went up into the eighties. The baby, healthy and contented, growing rapidly, did not like the heat, and Sue retreated to the air-conditioned nursery. Chris swam and sunbathed, soaking up the sun like a leopard, and

Cathy went on trying to work, her doors and windows wide open to catch the faint breeze.

She was finding it very difficult to concentrate. She felt tense and restless, unable to settle. She told herself it was the heat, but the barn was cool with its thick old walls. From the pool the harsh sensual voices of Chris' favourite singers, Elmore James, B.B.King, John Fogerty, Eric Burdon, Robert Plant, swelled in the quiet air, penetrating the barn with waves of turbulent feeling, until she could stand it no longer.

She threw down her brushes angrily and stalked out to the pool, and stood over Chris wrathfully, deafened by Eric Clapton's screaming guitar and agonised voice: '*Layla, you've got me on my knees!*'

Chris, lying on his stomach, looked up at her, grinning maliciously. 'Hello, Cathy, come for a swim?'

'Is it really necessary to have the music this loud? You're doing it on purpose. I can hear it in the barn all the time *and I can't think!*'

He rolled over, turning the volume down, and lay back, folding his arms under his head. He smiled up at her. 'You sure it's the music disturbing you, Cathy?'

She walked away, flushing. 'You'd better put something on. Mrs. Kaye will be bringing out the lunch soon.' And heard him laugh derisively.

He reached for a towel, wrapped it around his hips and followed her into the barn. 'You know who the real Layla was? The wife of Eric's best friend, George Harrison.'

Cathy shrugged angrily. She took out a whole section of the painting with turps and a clean rag, her hand shaking.

He sat propped on the window sill, watching her. 'You'll ruin it.'

'I don't care!'

A bee buzzed in through the window and out through the door. Chris said, abruptly, 'It's finished between you and Dev, Cathy.'

Her hand stopped, the pain flooding through her. 'He asked you to tell me?'

'No. But it is over, isn't it?'

She took a long, slow breath. After a moment she said, bitterly, 'It didn't last long did it? That woman Dev was in love with before me, the great love of his life, he was faithful to *her* for years.'

'Charis?'

Cathy hung the rag over her easel very carefully and turned round.

'*Charis* was Dev's girl?'

'Dev's *lady*,' Chris corrected. 'They were together two years. I thought you knew.'

'I didn't know it was *Charis*.'

'Yeah, a real heavy scene. She took everything, played him like a fish on a line and got bored. But Dev was crazy about her. He wanted to marry her.'

'But...Isn't she on drugs? An addict?'

Chris laughed shortly. 'Right. She's also very rich, exciting, and hot as hell in bed.'

Cathy began to clean her palette mechanically. Charis was Dev's mysterious heiress, mentioned in the biographies. It seemed obvious now. And she had gone with them on the Far East tour. He was seeing her all the time in London. The love of his life. He had never got over her.

Chris came over and put his arms around her.

'Don't look like that, love. I can't stand it.'

He drew her back close against him and pressed his lips into the hollow of her neck.

'I'm so in love with you, Cathy.'

'No.'

'You want me too. I can feel your heart banging against my hands.' He had opened her shirt and jeans and was caressing her body, turning her, kissing her neck, her mouth.

'It's been a long time since Dev, and you're very turned on, aren't you Cathy?'

She could not stop trembling. 'Please, Chris, don't...'

'Kiss me, Cathy.'

What did it matter? *Charis was Dev's lady.* She put her arms around Chris' neck and kissed him. His arms tightened, pulling her hard against him. She kissed him again, opening her mouth for him, surrendering.

'No wonder the painting is taking so long to finish,' said Dev's voice, dryly. He was leaning against the door frame, watching them. He came into the room and sat on Cathy's painting stool. He was very white. 'The old three-cornered triangle. Almost a joke. Husband, wife and best friend. But I didn't think it hurt this much.'

Chris said, his voice shaking, 'It doesn't hurt as much as not being married to her, Dev. Not being the father of her child.'

'You warned me a long time ago you'd take her off me if you could.' Dev closed his eyes. 'I just hoped she wouldn't ever want to go. I've been crazy. You could have told me, Cathy.'

Cathy clutched her shirt around her, feeling sick. 'Dev – it's not like you think.'

'I don't want to talk about it. Not yet.'

'You've got to listen. You can't go away thinking...'

'I *saw* you, Cathy. Very passionate. No pulling away. No sickness. Your body melting into his.' He got up quickly and went to the door. 'We're due in town to sign contracts, Chris. Are you coming?'

Chris did not move. He looked at Cathy.

'You need to change.' Dev waited.

Cathy turned away to the window. Chris hesitated a moment longer, then he went out with Dev.

Chapter Thirteen

Cathy had been painting for four days now, deep into the night and through the next day, stopping only to throw herself on the divan for a few hours sleep.

She knew it was the best thing she had ever done. More than a painting. A celebration of music and a way of life. The great joint portrait was finished at last, painted with love and understanding.

She came back slowly from the deep places she had been and remembered drearily that nothing was solved. Bill Hopkins had telephoned to say Dev was staying in town, and he had been away a week when she had re-started the painting. But now she could hear voices in the pool. So Dev was back, with friends. She hoped it was someone she knew and liked. Someone who would help to bridge over the awkward places, and then, perhaps, he might listen. She wondered where Chris was.

She cleaned her brushes and palette, threw away dirty paint rags, wiped her paint table and set out the tubes of paint for the next painting, taking her time. After a while, with nothing left to do, she let herself out of the heavy door. She walked around the corner of the barn and glanced casually through the arch in the tall hedge surrounding the pool. And stopped dead. After a while she took a deep, uneven breath and walked through the archway.

Dev and Dave Hampton were sitting on the side of the pool, their feet in the water. At the far end of the pool Tom Gibbon was playing chess with Bill Hopkins. And in the pool there were two girls, a blonde and a redhead, very beautiful and sexy in the bottom halves only of tiny bikinis.

Cathy watched them, motionless. She should have felt angry. But she felt only a cold emptiness. An inevitability. The disloyalty and breaking of trust had finally happened, just as she had always known it would.

One of the girls caught sight of her and burst out laughing. She called, in a high, brittle voice, 'I say, Paul, look what got in through your security fence.'

Cathy standing on the edge of the pool saw her reflection. She was wearing a filthy teeshirt and jeans. She was barefoot. Her hair, pinned up days ago, was half-falling down and she was very dirty, her face and arms spattered with paint.

The other girl looked around and laughed too. 'I thought hippies went out with Jimi Hendrix!

Cathy stared at them, feeling dazed and disconnected in the bright sunlight.

Dave Hampton got up, came round the pool and kissed her. 'Been working?'

'Four days, if this is Friday.' She smiled at him, uncertainly. 'I didn't know Dev was back. Have you been here long? You know I'm a bad hostess. Are you staying? Have you got a room?'

'Earlier this afternoon. I've got a room.'

'Who are they?'

He shrugged. 'Pick-ups.'

'Yours or Dev's?'

He hesitated, his eyes wary. 'They were at Knebworth last night.'

She had forgotten the big Knebworth Concert. Dev had asked her to go. For a moment she felt guilty, then she remembered that the quarrel about Chris had changed everything.'

'Aren't you going to introduce us, darling?' called the redhead.

Dave ignored her. 'Can I see the painting?'

'Whenever you like.'

Dev swam across the pool, pulled himself up and sat on the edge. 'Go on, Cathy, introduce yourself to my friends, Jilly and Samantha.'

She looked at him. Treachery. Disloyalty. 'What are they doing here?'

'They're, er, house guests.' He leaned back on his elbows, smiling unpleasantly, and she saw that he had been drinking, and his reckless desperation was back, worse than ever.

She said, quietly, 'In the Square – you made a solemn promise. You said you wouldn't bring girls to our home.'

'You made *me* a promise. In Church. On the Bible. *Forsaking all others.*'

'Who is she?' called the blonde, sulkily.

'Go on, tell her, Cathy,' he taunted. 'You'll be surprised, Jilly, you really will.'

She stared into the water and saw again the dejected figure. She felt ashamed in front of the beautiful girls with the splendid tanned bodies and long legs, like a sun-tan cream advertisement. And then, suddenly she remembered the painting on the easel in the barn, and straightened slowly. She was a person. A woman. Not a pretty doll belonging to Dev.

She began to pull the pins out of her hair and shook back the silky gold. The two girls, holding the rail below, watched her. Despite the dirty jeans and bare feet and the dark rings round her eyes, she was somehow impressive.

'Go on, give them a laugh. Tell them who you are.' He was trying to humiliate her in front of everyone, Cathy thought. Tom Gibbon had stopped playing chess and had turned to listen.

She put her head up and looked straight at Dev. 'I'm the mother of his son.'

There was a tense silence. He said, bitterly, 'Go on, fill in the minor details.'

Cathy looked at him blankly. Then she laughed, ice falling into a glass. She looked at each of the girls.

'I'm a painter. I have a studio here. I'm Catherine Harlow.'

Dev sprang to his feet, white with rage. 'Catherine Devlin, you little bitch. Catherine Devlin, *my wife.'*

One of the girls looked red, the other, scared. 'What...?'

'Meet your hostess,' said Tom Gibbon, grinning. 'Dev's wife.' He was clearly enjoying the drama.

Cathy turned stiffly and walked into the house.

Painter, not wife. *Painter.* Her brain repeated the word again and yet again as she walked steadily up to her room. It was all over. *You don't have to stay forever,* the boy had said.

Dev had no real interest in the girls, she thought. It was just his cruel way of breaking up the marriage and getting rid of her. She should have had more courage. She should have left months ago, after the concert, instead of hanging around until he humiliated her and destroyed her pride. She was free to go now.

The baby.

She would have to leave the baby too.

The realisation flooded over her sickeningly. She sat down on the bed, shivering, feeling the cold sweat running down her body.

Impossible to paint full-time and look after the baby properly. Impossible to pay for a lodging and a nursery nurse with the money she would earn.

She could not go. But how could she stay here, to become the butt of contemptuous jokes, humiliated and degraded by a succession of Dev's girls, while he enjoyed his revenge. Even her mother hadn't had to put up with that. Better to be alone and have some self-respect. If she stayed she would not work again. The hatred and resentment would eat away at her, destroying her ability to paint once more.

The choice was clear – stay with the baby, living in Dev's house, shamed and abject, dying of the corrosive poison of hatred, or leave the baby and try to find freedom to do her work and grow as a person.

The baby needed her. He would fret...

She laughed harshly. Not true. He had scarcely seen her these last weeks as she worked for her exhibition. There were so many people to care for him. Sue and Mrs. Kaye were the important people in his life. And Dev too. He loved Dev.

She would have to leave him. She had to go. She could not give up her work, live without her painting. Perhaps Dev would let her see the baby sometimes.

She pulled her old suitcase from a wall cupboard and opened it on the bed, but still she hesitated. She opened the drawers and stared into them, not seeing the contents, her hands shaking, unable to take the first steps, pain wrenching her stomach.

She couldn't do it. It was impossible to leave the baby. She would take him with her and try to cope somehow.

She went along to the nursery, and found Sue and Paul in the daffodil yellow bathroom attached to the nursery suite. Sue was leaning over the baby bath, laughing and tickling his tummy. The baby was shrieking with laughter and thumping the water with his fists to make it splash. As she watched, Sue lifted him and wrapped him in a huge fleecy towel, and saw Cathy standing silent in the doorway.

'Is anything the matter, Mrs. Devlin?'

Cathy turned into the nursery. His toys were scattered over the floor. She picked up a big blue rabbit from the soft yellow carpet and put it into the play pen, along with the piles of toys Dev had bought for him.

The late afternoon sun was streaming in through the big open windows. Cathy closed the window and pulled the white and yellow curtains close, staring across the quiet fields to the distant blue hills.

How could she take him away from all this, to a grotty one-room lodging in the dirt and noise of London?

Dev would never let him go. He would use his money and influence and fight it through the courts. He would take him out of the country if necessary, and she would never see the baby again. Just another tug-of-love case, destroying the baby's security and happiness, ruining their own lives with hatred.

'Kiss Mummy goodnight,' said Sue, bringing the baby across to her.

His spun gold hair was combed into a quiff, and he was rosy in his cotton nightshirt, printed with Jungle Book characters. Cathy held the small waving hand between her finger and thumb and stroked it gently. The baby pulled away impatiently and flung both arms around Sue's neck, hugging her and burrowing his face against her neck.

'He's shy,' Sue said, embarrassed.

Cathy stared at them, white, feeling cold and empty. There was always a price, Caleb had said. She had never guessed it would be so high.

Sue looked at her, puzzled. 'Are you feeling all right, Mrs. Devlin?'

'Look after him. Keep him safe, Sue.' She kissed the baby's soft cheek.

She went back to her room and began packing her small stock of working clothes and toilet things. It took very little time. She left the fur coat and the clothes Dev had bought for her. One of the things that had made him very angry was her refusal to spend any of the money, which was pouring into the joint account from the recent tour.

'It's not my money!'

'Okay,' Dev sneered, 'Look like an unemployed labourer if you want.'

'That's what I am,' Cathy said. 'Better than a Sindy doll.'

When she had finished packing, she showered, washed and dried her hair and changed into a shirt and a clean pair of jeans. Then taking her short jacket she carried her case down to the entrance hall. She was relieved to find it deserted. They were still at the pool, enjoying the evening sun. She wanted to avoid arguments and scenes. Nothing anybody could say now would change her mind. She could see her course quite clearly.

Painter, not wife.

She phoned for a taxi. At least she had some of her own money now, carefully put away from the sales of the June exhibition. Enough for a room somewhere for a few months, until she could sell some more work. Peace, quiet. Away from this place where pain waited like mines in a field, stopping her working. Freedom at last.

When she saw the taxi turning into the drive, she went back to the barn, threw brushes and paints into her old straw bag. She took the painting off the easel and leaned it against the wall, face inward, so that it would be protected from the dust. She looked at the rack of completed paintings, calculating the size of the van needed to collect them for the October exhibition, and then she left, locking the door after her.

She felt icy, without emotion, her brain brilliantly clear.

The girls were still shrieking in the water. Dev lay on an airbed, looking bored. She walked back along the side of the pool and paused briefly in front of him, not knowing what to say. He looked at her expressionlessly. Then he raised himself slowly on his elbow and saw the old straw bag. His eyes widened with understanding and disbelief.

'I'll send an address when I have one. For the div...lawyers. Please look after the baby, Dev. Please don't let girls like that near him.'

'Cathy...' Dev's colour drained away. '*Cathy!'*

But already she had gone, and a few moments later the taxi door slammed and the sound of the engine faded away up the drive.

Chapter Fourteen

Caleb Crow found her a flat. It was around the corner from the Arundell Gallery, six floors up, at the very top of an old Victorian office block. It was unfurnished and incredibly expensive, but Caleb had advanced her some money on the strength of the commissions from the June exhibition and it was a place to work.

It had one very large light room and a small room at the back with sink and fridge and a cooker brown with grease and rust. There was a landing cupboard for storage and, one floor below, an ancient bathroom shared with the office on that floor. But Cathy was the only one who used the old bathtub, dignified, on four Queen Anne shell legs and with enormous brass taps. After six o'clock everyone had gone home and the building and the surrounding streets were deserted, left to the pigeons and the water carts.

For the first time in her life she was truly on her own and free, but she was suddenly afraid that she would not be able to look after herself. Living with Dev seemed to have sapped her confidence badly. She did not mind being alone in the flat, but when she thought of the money she had borrowed and had to repay by her own efforts there was a hollow feeling in her stomach.

After the free-flowing extravagance of Cox's Farm it was difficult to deal with the money. She forgot to buy things like soap and loo paper, and ran out of basic foods in the middle of the week, and had to live on eggs and lettuce. Most of her money went on paints and canvases, and there was nothing left for magazines and books and new shoes. Money was a very good reason for getting married, after all, Cathy thought. Nobody ever said so, but people who were married always had a better standard of living than single people.

She had bought the essentials – a divan, bed linen, a long table to draw and eat at, some second-hand chairs, china, saucepans. She cleaned the cooker and hung her clothes from a broom handle across the corner of the room, but she could not bring herself to fix up the place properly. She told herself she did not want to waste her small savings, but the real reason was that she did not want the flat to seem too permanent, too settled. Dev would probably telephone. Perhaps they could talk properly and reach some sort of agreement. Somehow she could not believe the marriage was truly over.

She wandered around miserably, waiting for the phone to ring and took long walks in the dusty, sunset streets, too unsettled and too unhappy to start painting. She had sent her address and telephone number to Dev. Surely he would phone, surely he would want to talk, make some sort of arrangements? But no calls or letters came.

The loss of the baby was agony. Now she was away from him she realised how deep and close the ties had become. She worried about him during the day, and woke in the night hearing him crying. She could not relax until she had telephoned Mrs. Kaye each day to make sure he was all right. Mrs. Kaye was very patient and understanding. 'Ring any time,' she said, '*Any* time. I can guess how you feel. I'm so sorry you couldn't get along together. He kicked those hussies out straight away you know. Perhaps later on...'

'Perhaps,' said Cathy, non-committally.

She had expected to *feel* free, but there were too many unresolved problems, too many loose ends. Freedom was a long way away.

When she realised, one day, how much time she was wasting, mooning around, waiting for Dev to call or phone, she was so furious with herself that she went out and spent too much on things for the flat – a striking orange and blue rug, some deep orange curtains – determined to make it a real home. She painted the walls of the small back room a cheerful orangey-gold.

Gradually the panic and agony lessened, but she still telephoned Mrs. Kaye each day, and she still listened for the sound of the telephone and ran to answer it, even though she knew now it was not likely to be Dev.

Chris telephoned regularly for several weeks, but she put the receiver down each time and left it off the hook. Once, when she came back to the flat, she found him waiting in his car outside and walked away quickly before he saw her. She slept on Caleb's sofa that night, and eventually Chris stopped ringing.

She tried to pick up the threads of her old life, but Nick and Alun had passed their finals and left London, and there were new people she did not know at Hamilton Square. The Principal of the London College of Art said he could not accept an application for re-entry in September. He might accept it for the following year, but why didn't she try Camberwell or Goldsmiths instead?

Julie too had passed her finals, but she was still in London. She had married Ray, her fiancé, very quietly, and was running her own fashion business. She was grateful to Cathy, insisting that it was the publicity of the wedding dress, which had started her off. A businessman had seen the dress in the paper and made her an offer of finance.

When they met for lunch one day, Julie looked surprisingly sophisticated and chic. She was cheerful, excited about the opportunities offered. She did not mention Chris, or her husband, but chattered on about the successes and problems of her new business, and Cathy wondered if it was a cover-up for deeper feelings.

At last, when they were standing on the pavement outside the restaurant, Cathy said, 'Julie, are you happy?

You know – married to Ray. After the way you were with Chris...'

Julie looked away. 'It's all right. We know each other so well. He helps me with the business, but I don't see him much as a matter of fact. I'm madly busy and I have to be at the workshop very late.'

Cathy said, bitterly, 'Those two really did for us, didn't they?'

Julie's eyes were hard and brilliant. 'Nobody gets everything they want, Cathy. And I'm going to be the Mary Quant of the century. You'll see! What about you? Your exhibition is in October, isn't it? I suppose you're working frantically to get as much done as possible now you've got away from Dev.'

Cathy stared at the pavement, ashamed. 'I've got some ideas.'

'Do you mean you haven't started yet? Cathy, it's a fantastic opportunity. Don't mess it up. Only the very best get a show at the Arundell.'

'I don't think I'm good enough.'

Julie looked at her and then laughed aloud. 'Marriage didn't do anything for your confidence, Cathy. You know you're a marvellous painter. A genius probably. You've got things to do, Cathy. Stop worrying and get on with them. I must go!'

She hailed a taxi, and opened its door. 'I found the secret. *Work.* It's the most important thing. The most satisfying and permanent. Better than people.' The door slammed and the cab moved off, leaving Cathy staring after it. She went home, telephoned Caleb about the portrait commissions, and began to stretch a large canvas.

In the next few months Cathy worked harder than she thought possible. Her personal unhappiness was not obvious in her work, but her portraits had a new depth and compassion, a maturity that had not been there before.

The commissions, completed, brought in more commissions, especially from the musicians and singers she had met with Dev. They enjoyed having their portraits painted, and it began to be fashionable among the rock stars to own a Cathy Harlow portrait. She had more work than she could take on.

Two chalk studies of baby Paul in the June exhibition had also brought requests for drawings of children, but Cathy found excuses not to do them, although they paid very well. She still could hardly bring herself to look at small babies. The loss of baby Paul did not seem to get easier to bear. She was losing the precious days of his babyhood. She didn't dare ask to see him, knowing that if she went back to the Farm she would not find the courage to leave again.

Instead, she painted the hairdresser on the corner, mirrors reflecting mirrors in endless space, her face a white mask. She painted the cleaning lady of the offices below, her dark head thrown back, laughing, merging into the chocolate brown walls and the dark pools of water on the floor.

She worked all day and most of the night, and when she could work no more because of her sore eyes, she walked the empty streets. Julie was right. Work was the answer. It reduced the pain to a manageable size.

Apart from the people who came to sit for their portraits, Cathy had few visitors. Caleb Crow came occasionally – to keep an eye on his investment, he said – but really, Cathy suspected, to provoke and disturb her, so that she worked with an angry brilliance. Caleb didn't think complacency was good for young painters.

'I hear Dev's hitting the high spots and the vodka.'

'Who told you?'

'Tom Gibbon. *Burning up,* he said. You going back to him?'

Cathy gave a ghost of a laugh. 'He hasn't asked. He's glad to be rid of me.'

Caleb regarded her shrewdly. 'You know, I feel sorry for Dev.'

Her control gave way a little. '*Sorry! I'm* the injured party. You don't know what he did to me.'

'I know he needed his head examining when he picked on you to marry. Anyone with half an eye could see you're ruthless. Men are bloody fools, the way they underrate women. It's all that luscious exterior. Soft as a pillow – on the outside.' He laughed. 'A chocolate-covered hand grenade. I never knew a painter with your obsession, Cathy, who wouldn't swop their grandmother for a tube of paint.'

Cathy said, tightly, 'I am not obsessed.'

'You're not only obsessed. You're addicted. The arts are addictive, Cathy. You're an art junkie. Even more ruthless than your old man where your work is concerned – even if your long gold hair *is* hanging down.'

Cathy was offended and angry. 'I'm not ruthless. I put people first.'

Caleb snorted derisively and stamped to the door. 'You left Dev, didn't you? Why? Because you couldn't live together – or because it interfered with your painting and you wanted to be free?'

'How can I be free? You just said I'm addicted,' Cathy snapped, sulkily.

'That's your problem, woman. You're going to have trouble working that out.'

'I've worked it out. I'm free *now*.' Her voice sounded too defiant.

He laughed. 'Ruthless.'

'*I am not...*'

He said, cruelly, 'You left your kid, too, didn't you?'

It took Cathy a long while to get over Caleb's visits. They were blessedly infrequent, but to her surprise Dave Hampton came regularly. He was making an album in a studio a few streets away, and he got into the habit of dropping in late at night after the recording session. He brought wine and stayed for an hour or two, watching her paint.

'You're the only person I know still up at two in the morning and sober,' he said grinning. 'When do you sleep?'

'When I need it. I don't need much though.'

She drew him sprawled on the old sofa she had found in a junk shop, his head against the back, eyes closed, muscles stiff with exhaustion. A long way from the vivid energy of *Hampton at Azras*.

'I like it here. Private. Quiet. Female company.' He opened his eyes and smiled at her.

'Don't tell me you're lonely, Dave!'

He slid his finger down the side of the wine glass, intent. 'Sometimes I'm so bloody lonely it hurts. You know I've broken up with Janey?'

'But surely – you know – you're in a band. You're a star. All those girls screaming for you.'

'It's nice, but they don't mean a lot. Not after Janey. Hangers-on. Strangers. Not the people you really want.'

'But what about the other members of the band? Your friends.'

'It's okay when we're on the road. I feel all right then, but when we're at home I'm at a loose end. My best friend, Ronnie Craig, he's in the band. We write all our songs together. He's married. Nice house in Esher. I stay sometimes but it's kind of painful to see them together. With the baby. Brings it back like it was with Janey. Although we didn't have a baby, of course.'

Cathy did not want to talk about babies. 'What about your bass player, Mike Adams? He's Janey's brother, isn't he? Is he married too?'

'No. I moved in with him for a while, after the break up. But it didn't work out. He blames me for it. Blames me for letting Janey throw herself away on Jay Bird.' He looked at Cathy, letting her read his anguish. 'He's ruined her life. Destroyed her career.'

Cathy was surprised. 'But every time you put on the television she's there. The radio too. What is it this week – number six, or something. She's a great star. I really want to paint her.'

'Number three and rising. It'll be another number one. But all the same he has ruined her. She's not a pop singer. She's got a fantastic operatic voice, and acting ability too. Another Callas, or better, maybe. At her age she ought to be in Italy, studying, building a repertoire. But Jay Bird won't let her go. She always swore she wouldn't sell out to pop, but she lets Jay Bird stop her.' He sounded bitter.

'Perhaps she doesn't want to go any more.'

'She wants to go all right. They row about it. I don't know why she stays with him. She has a hell of a time.' His voice was harsh. 'Mike tells me all about it. It's a good way of getting back at me.'

Cathy was appalled. Seeing into other people's private hells did nothing to help her own. Pain and despair seemed everywhere. 'I'm sorry. I didn't realised you've had such a bad time.'

'Having.'

'Success? The Big Time?'

'It helps, but not as much as you'd think in the long run.'

Cathy was silent, remembering a similar conversation with Chris. *Suppose work and success could not fill all the lonely gaps?*

'I thought you knew about me. That Azra painting, when Janey and I were breaking up, you got it all. All the desperation. All the savagery. I could have killed someone that night. Nearly did in the riot. And playing with Dev. The music was fantastic. One of the biggest highs of my entire life. All those tearing emotions mixed up. When I saw your painting, I couldn't believe it.'

Cathy was remembering that night too. Suddenly, with an actual, physical pain, she longed to put her arms around Dev and hug him. She put her palette down with unsteady hands and started to clean the mixing area carefully. Too carefully. Dev, swinging her round, holding her tight against him, kissing her.

'Cathy?' Dave's voice was suddenly sharp. 'Cathy, are you all right? You're not crying?'

'No. I was thinking.'

He looked at her closely. 'Listen, when did you eat last? Come on. Get your coat. Let's go find an all-night cafe for a good nosh-up.'

Cathy laughed at the old London word and felt better. They went out, arm-in-arm, and later as they sat close together at the back of the cafe, neither of them noticed the photographer focussing his miniature camera. But the photograph in the newspapers next day set off a chain of reaction.

Dev beat up a newsman who dared to ask questions and then went in search of a man he knew who could supply happy oblivion with something stronger than vodka. Chris Carter stared at the picture, motionless, for several minutes, and then went to see Janey Adams. And later, Janey Adams stopped her recording session and went home with a splitting headache.

T-Zers in the *NME* said: *Seen fading into the wallpaper of Sidi's Curry House at two o'clock in the morning, Paul Devlin's missing missus, Cathy, snuggling up to Hot Hot*

Hot Dave Hampton of Night Mission out for a quick snack
between sessions, no doubt.

Cathy did not see the photograph or the paragraph and
Dave did not tell her.

It was a week later that, bring her back to the flat, he
kissed her in the shadows of the deep Victorian porch. It
was a good kiss, expert, and he was very attractive, but
Cathy felt nothing. After a while he let he go.

'It's no good, is it?'

'Not really. Not for you, either.'

He smiled at her crookedly. 'You have to go on trying.'

'I like you, Dave. I like you so much, but...but I'm not
Janey.'

'And I'm not Dev.'

Cathy said, hostile, 'Who says I want Dev?'

'Chris, then.'

'*No.*'

He smiled again, watching her. 'Who are you trying to
fool, Cathy?'

Chapter Fifteen

The commission to paint a portrait of Janey Adams came out of the blue.

Cathy had given up any hope of hearing from her, and she was very excited. She was also shy and nervous. Janey Adams was such a big star, almost a legend, with so many chart successes to her credit, and her own weekly television show at peak viewing time. Everything Dave had said had made her want to meet Janey.

She arrived, incongruously, on a motorbike in leathers and a helmet, explaining that she used the bike because in London it got her from place to place quickly, and people did not recognise her in motorcycle gear. She said she found all the publicity and fan worship difficult to handle, and Cathy, surprised, warmed to her and relaxed.

Janey was dramatically dark, with clear olive skin, tilted dark eyes, and thick, heavy dark hair. She moved gracefully, and her long slender hands, their movements as precise and expressive as a mime artist, fascinated Cathy.

On her television show Janey seemed very sure of herself, warm, extrovert, sensuous, but off screen, she was quiet, serious, only a little older than Cathy herself. She was not exactly withdrawn or shy, but turned inwards, Cathy thought, very controlled, as though there were a lot of strong feelings locked away, which might break through and be too much for everyone. Cathy remembered then, Janey singing the blues at the presentation, and the tears running down her face.

She said, staring at Cathy, 'I saw you at the Awards party, but we didn't speak.'

'I was too shy, and then you had to sing.' They were both silent, remembering. Cathy said, 'I'm a fan. I heard you sing once at the Blues Room. You were marvellous. I've wanted to paint you ever since.'

Janey was surprised. 'That was my first professional engagement.'

'You were wearing a pink dress. Very daring. Low cut. My boy friend couldn't take his eyes off you. I was really fed up, and wishing I had enough courage to wear something like that, until you started to sing and then I didn't think of anything else.'

'You'd never believe the trouble that dress made for me!'

They smiled at each other, and suddenly everything was changed. Warmth, understanding, sympathy, *friendship,* flowed between them.

'The way I work,' Cathy said, 'I'm just going to sit and stare at you for a long time. Not drawing. Just looking. I use a kind of meditation, an Eastern method. You can move about. Talk. Do what you want. When I start to draw I might ask you to keep still for a while then. I make a lot of drawings before I begin to paint.'

Janey changed into a long black dress, sewn with silver beads. The dress, slit to the hip, flowed around her as she moved, transformed at last into the exciting superstar.

'Is this all right? Jay thought I ought to be painted in this dress. It has a kind of sentimental value. I wore it the night I sang *Moonlight Girl* at Wembley and had my first big hit.'

She stared at her mirror-image sombrely, combing out her heavy hair, and met Cathy's eyes in the mirror, strangely defensive. 'I was with Night Mission. I used to help my brother Mike with the band.'

'I've seen them,' said Cathy. 'They're brilliant. Dave Hampton.'

Janey moved away, her back to Cathy. 'We were together, you know.'

'Yes, Dave said. But you married Jay Bird of the Bird Lovers.' She could not keep the hostility out of her voice.

Janey turned and looked at her. 'Dave comes here?'

'Sometimes.'

'I don't want...'

'It's all right. He comes after sessions usually. Very late.'

Janey went to the window and stared down. 'He comes often?'

'Yes,' said Cathy, honestly. 'We get on well. Sometimes we have a meal together.'

There was a long silence. Janey said abruptly, 'I knew anyway. That's why I came here. To see *you*. To see Dave's new girl. I suppose I hoped it would cure me. Make it real and final.'

'How did you know?'

'The picture of you and Dave in the paper.'

'I didn't see it,' Cathy said, indifferently. 'I don't care now what's in the papers.'

'Chris Carter came to the studios, especially to show me. All smiling and silky smooth like a panther. *'I've got a nice little surprise for you, love. What are you going to do about it?'* Her fingers tightened on the window sill. 'One day I'll kill Chris Carter. As though it's anything to do with me now. I've no right to say who Dave sees, what he does. I'm *married*. I can't keep him chained.'

'I'm sorry if it upsets you,' Cathy said. 'Dave's a friend of Dev and Chris and he used to come to the Farm.'

'I don't want to know. It's too painful.' She leaned her head against the window and closed her eyes.

Cathy said, gently, 'We don't...I mean, he's just a friend, Janey. I'm not Dave's new girl.'

'He's free to do as he wants.'

'Is he? You know how he feels about you. He hasn't changed.'

Janey's voice was hard. 'Dave likes girls. He wouldn't live like a monk. And you're too beautiful.'

Cathy said, tightly, holding her anger, 'It takes two. I'm not available.' Janey opened her eyes and stared at her. 'Look, I just got free. It took a long time and it *hurts*.

Maybe you don't know, but I had to leave my baby as well.
I need my freedom more than anything. Freedom to be a
person. Freedom to *work*. I don't want to be – *connected.*'

'I'm sorry,' Janey said, at last. 'I didn't think. I didn't
understand.'

Cathy shrugged and picked up her drawing board. She
clipped on new sheets of paper and started to draw. After a
while she said, 'I'm sorry I snapped. It's just – guilt – I
suppose.'

Janey sat down on the sofa, one leg tucked beneath her,
her arms spread along the back. She smiled at Cathy
ruefully.

'Freedom is what it's all about, isn't it? Girls get trapped
between what they want to do and how they feel about
people. They want to be free to do great things in the world,
but they meet a nice guy, and settle for him. Or sometimes
it's babies. They want a kid desperately. And it seems like
you can't have both.'

'You've got both,' Cathy said. 'Fame. A career. A
husband.'

Janey laughed shortly. 'Not the right career and not the
right man. But whatever you choose you're not free.
Choose the guy and the home and baby and you want
freedom, a career, *something else.* Choose the career, do
your thing, and you go on wanting the guy and the kid. I
don't think you're ever free, not really. Sometimes I wonder
if there's any such thing as freedom. It's all a big fix. You
can only be as free as your character lets you.' She laughed
again, grimly and quoted, 'Man is born free; and
everywhere he is in chains.' I think Rousseau meant actual
physical chains, poverty, political oppression, but you can
be chained in other ways. Mentally.

'Fear is what stops you being free. I used to be frightened
of everything. Making a fool of myself. Losing control.
Sex.'

Cathy could not believe what she had just heard, and looked up, startled, from her drawing. 'But you...you're...' She stumbled over the words, trying not to offend.

Janey said, ruefully, 'I know what you're trying to say. That I'm a half-naked pin-up poster in the men's locker room, and I must know everything, the way my body is, the way I sing, the way I move? But it's true. I was terrified of my sex feelings. Dave changed all that. Made me lose control. Once I'd let go I found it was all right. I could ride the wave. I was free.'

Cathy stared at the paper, not moving, thinking of her own fear and shame. Could you let go, ride the wave and still be free?

Janey said, watching her, 'If you love someone it's all right. It's lies and viciousness and violence and hate does the harm. Not sex.'

'Yes,' said Cathy. 'Violence kills everything. It spoiled everything between Dev and me.'

Janey got up and stretched. 'I have to go. I have to be in Leeds tonight.'

She slid into her tight leather trousers and motorcycle jacket, combed her hair swiftly and deftly in the mirror.

'I wish I could stay. It's peaceful here. No phone ringing. No screaming people. The first time I've relaxed in months. I could come again on Friday for the next sitting if that's all right.'

Cathy said, smiling, 'Feel free.' They both laughed. 'I mean, come whenever you want.'

'You mean that? You're not just being polite?'

'Come whenever you want to relax. I'm nearly always here. I'm like a rabbit. I only pop out for food.'

Janey laughed. 'I'll bring some carrots.'

After that, Janey came often, slipping away for an hour or two when she was in London and could escape the never-ending demands made on her – publicity, interviews, photo-sessions, rehearsals, signing autographs, costume fittings, hair, make-up, travelling, radio, television, concerts, even a film. She seemed to work twenty-four hours a day, hardly stopping. Cathy wondered how long she would be able to keep it up.

Sometimes Janey was so tired she fell asleep on the old sofa, at other times she would sit silently, her legs folded under her, her eyes abstracted, dreaming and waiting. But quite often she was so keyed up she could not even bear to sit, but wandered around the room, her long fingers delicately touching the few ornaments, the books, the jars of brushes, her voice brittle and desperate.

'What is it?' Cathy said. 'It might help if you talk.'

'It's Jay, my husband. As usual.' She wandered over to the window and stared down. 'He's a long term heroin addict. We talked about freedom once. And chains. Jay is chained to drugs. I found out just after we were married. He says he'll give it up. Take the cure. Then I get home from a gig and find him lying in a mess of yellow vomit.'

'I'm sorry.' It seemed a stupid and inadequate thing to say. 'I mean, it must be awful for you. But it's not hopeless is it? He seems so young and alive...With your help...'

Janey turned, the tears standing in her eyes. 'They give them five years. I'm not much use. I seem to make him worse. I'm not free either. He knows I've never got over Dave.

'Dave said once that being in love with him meant that I'd never be free again, and I hated that. I wanted to be free like you. I didn't want to make a commitment. I wanted to go to Italy and study opera. But he was right. If you love someone you're not free. I thought if we only lived together I'd be free to do what I wanted.'

Cathy said, 'You could go to Italy now if you really wanted to. What's stopping you?'

'You don't *want* to go any more. You don't want to be alone.'

Cathy said, 'I walked away. I got free.'

'Are you sure, Cathy?'

The sadness in her voice made Cathy angry. 'Are you saying girls can't be independent? That we've always got to lean on someone? Be looked after?'

'No. No, I don't mean that. You *are* independent. Self-sufficient. You do what you want and look after yourself. I just mean I feel somehow deep down that all human beings, men as well as women, are dependent on each other. What happens if you get too far out? Too alone? Too disconnected?'

Cathy stared at the canvas in front of her. 'I don't know. I can't answer that. Maybe I'll find out. All I know is I have to paint.' She laughed bleakly, hearing herself. 'I suppose I am ruthless. Caleb said so. He said I'm an art junkie. Addicted. I thought Dev stopped me being free but of course I wasn't free before I met him. I'll never be really free either. *I'm* chained to my need to paint. And I'm chained to fear. And resentment. I realised over the last few weeks that I haven't worked *anything* out. Not even my feelings about Dev.'

Janey said, 'You hate Dev, don't you? You never talk about him. You change the subject when I do.'

Cathy looked at her quickly. 'I don't hate him.'

'What's he done? I mean I know he's got faults. But I always liked Dev. What broke it up? Did he have other girls?'

'No. Yes. At least, I don't know. Maybe. But it wasn't that. It was...' She came to a stop.

'You don't want to talk about it. Forget it.'

'It's just that I find it difficult. It was...He...Well, it started all wrong and I never got over it. I just can't forget how it started. I'd only just left school. I didn't want to get married. I just wanted to paint and paint. I didn't want a baby. I resented it. Resented everything he made me do.

'I felt so bitter, Janey. Resentment is like corrosive acid. It burned away everything, even my painting. I couldn't paint. I couldn't let it go. I was frightened of Dev. Of being taken over. And he did too. Take me over, I mean. Like a dolly. And I was too frightened of everything to stop it.'

'Yes,' Janey admitted. 'Dev is frightening. I wouldn't like to get on his wrong side. Chris either. They're different. As though they come from another planet.' She grinned, looking at Cathy. 'You too. You're like this old Victorian print in our digs in Inverness. A girl standing in the wind in a high place, with a long cloak and her fair hair streaming out. And on her face there's this strange look, as though she's reading something in the wind. It's called *Second Sight.*'

Cathy smiled, watching her wriggling into her leathers. 'And you're a Klimt woman. Very opulent. You ought to be painted without clothes.'

Janey laughed and slapped the curves of her bottom. 'I'm getting fat. I have to watch my weight. One of these days I'll be a big fat prima donna...'

She shut off what she was saying and suddenly Cathy saw that her eyes were full of tears again. 'Oh hell and blast!' She brushed the tears away impatiently and zipped her jacket with its heavy collar. 'You *can* have both things you know. The guy and do your own thing. I'm sure you can. You just have to be patient. And tough. And canny. Maybe we don't start with freedom, but work *towards* it all our lives. How does that grab you?'

'Not a lot,' Cathy said, laughing.

Janey picked up her motorcycle helmet and went to the door. 'It's bloody difficult being a girl these days.'

'In the old days you would have been in the kitchen with three kids already.'

Janey turned, grinning wickedly, 'No, I'd have chosen the other profession. A discreet house in St. John's Wood, and musical evenings with Prince Teddy.'

'And mind-blistering boredom all the afternoon?'

'All right, you win. It's *marvellous* living in the late Nuclear Age, *darling!*'

The portrait was going well. Cathy had painted the great singing star, the romantic legend who could hold twenty thousand people still and silent with the power of her voice and personality.

Janey was standing, looking out of the canvas, her head back, her arms flung high, loving and loved. The dark dress slipped around her, transparent, hardly concealing the pale skin, stage moonlight glittering darkly on its silky folds and drifts of silver beads.

'I love it,' Janey said. 'But it's not *me*. It's what people think I am. Perhaps I should have worn something else. It's too romantic.'

'No, it's right. All the reflecting lights moving like water. A night goddess.'

Janey laughed but the laughter broke in the middle. After a moment she said, huskily, 'Dave said that once. He wrote that song for me, *Moonlight Girl.*'

Cathy said, 'You think about Dave all the time, don't you, Janey?'

She looked away. 'I didn't leave him, you know. He threw me out because of Jay.'

Cathy looked at her startled. 'Why on earth...?'

'I had a hit record. An easy success. I couldn't make up my mind about going to Italy and I didn't want to leave Dave. I thought he'd find someone else. And then I felt, oh, I don't know...trapped. As though it was Dave's fault. He kept on about getting married and starting a family. We

rowed all the time. I had so much work...And than I had the
chance of going to the States with Jay and his band.

'Dave didn't want me to go. I didn't want to go either,
really, but I thought I'd show him I was independent. And
then there was the money. And Jay. I had no idea it could
be like that. Dave warned me about being on the road. He
had this thing about Jay. I suppose he guessed I had special
feelings about him...Even Ronnie warned me...Well, when I
got back to England, Dave threw me out.'

There was a long silence. Janey took a deep breath. 'I
was stupid. I took some sleeping pills. Jay found me and
took me to hospital. He saved my life and I married him. I
love him, Cathy. Not as much as Dave. But he's very
sexual. I'm really hooked. I couldn't leave him. Not free.'

She looked at Cathy, trying to smile. 'This must sound
incredible to you. Being in love with two people.'

'No,' said Cathy. She began to mix a dark plum colour on
her palette. 'I know how you feel.'

Janey watched her hand shaking and said, slowly, awed,
'Not *Chris*, as well as Dev?'

Cathy worked dark green into the plum, and did not
answer.

Janey laughed briefly. 'Well, at least you didn't make the
mistake of choosing the wrong one.'

Cathy's brush stopped. The silence stretched and cracked
with tension. At last she looked at Janey directly. Her grey-
violet eyes were like stone. 'I didn't choose at all. Dev
forced me to have sex. I got pregnant.'

Janey sat up, shocked. 'Cathy!'

'That's what was behind all that beautiful romance the
papers thought up. I was painting at Cox's Farm.
Trespassing, although I didn't know that. Dev and Chris
found me and made me go back to the house with them. We
had food and a lot to drink. They had just come back from a
long tour in the States and were high, crazy with exhaustion

and booze. I had too much to drink too. Then Dev took me outside and... and made me have sex.'

'He thought you wanted it,' Janey said, ironically. 'That's what they all say, isn't it?'

'I don't know. I don't understand anything about it. We've never really talked about it. It's all mixed up.'

'What happened?'

'When I got pregnant I had nowhere to go. Nothing to live on. Dev found me and wanted the baby. Everybody said I ought to marry him – my family, friends, *everybody*. Because of the money. And there was the future of the baby.'

'An abortion?'

Cathy shook her head and closed her eyes. 'I couldn't.'

'You didn't love Dev at all?'

Cathy hesitated. She said at last, 'In the beginning maybe. We danced and I wanted him. The first time I ever felt like that. But the violence and fear killed it. I was so frightened. It was the first time you see. I can't talk about it usually. You're different.'

'You ought not to have married him,' said Janey, uncompromisingly.

'It's easy to say that now. But then I couldn't see any way out. They threw me out of my college course. I couldn't earn enough to keep both of us. You know most girls don't have enough money to live as they want.'

After a while Janey said, slowly, 'Where does Chris fit in? The grapevine says he's crazy about you.'

Cathy was surprised. 'Who...?'

'It's a terrible gossipy business. When you left Dev, why didn't you go to Chris? And don't tell me you don't fancy him. We all do. He only has to walk in a room and the women fall apart.'

Cathy said, 'Chris isn't the nice easy relaxed guy people think. He's tough and clever and he plays people like a chess game. And he's dangerous. More than Dev even.'

'I know,' said Janey, unexpectedly. 'All that tamped down sex power.'

Cathy pushed the paint aimlessly around the centre of the palette. 'I couldn't forget Dev with Chris. They're so close. They've always been together. They're like one person almost. They even know what each other are thinking.' Her voice shook. 'We all do, Janey. It's horrible.'

She flung down her palette, wiped her fingers on a rag and said, abruptly, 'I can't do any more now.'

Chapter Sixteen

In late October, Cathy's one-woman exhibition opened at the Arundell Gallery, with a glittering Private View, full of famous rock faces.

Many people thought the superb portrait of Janey Adams was outstanding, but most agreed that the huge joint painting of Dev and Chris at Wembley was Cathy's masterpiece. The two canvases were cleated together for ease of transport. Dev and Chris, silver, were caught in a cage of silver beams, crossing and crisscrossing, striking reflections off their instruments, so they seemed trapped in a glistening web of light and sound. Space lords, remote, beautiful, imprisoned by their glittering life.

Caleb hung it on the end wall of the gallery alone, picked out with cool spotlights. It was astonishingly beautiful, glinting iridescent in pearl and silver greys, and people drew in their breath when they looked at it.

The other paintings and studies from Cox's Farm were there too. Caleb had sent a van for them a few weeks before and Cathy moved among them staring critically. She felt she had already moved on, leaving them far behind. But Caleb was grunting more than usual, and she supposed he was satisfied. She did not look at the chalk studies of baby Paul, surrounded all evening by crowds of cooing admirers. They were the first to be sold, all gone in the first hour.

The evening spun past, a jigsaw of congratulations, known and unknown faces. Cathy saw Dave Hampton, white, staring at Janey's portrait, and Julie was there with Alun, who had come up from Wales. She had insisted on making Cathy a new dress for the opening. It was a transparent smoky-violet fabric, like cobwebs, over grey silk, with a high neck and full sleeves.

'Still trying to turn me into a faery lady, Julie?' Cathy laughed.

Julie grinned back. 'You *are* a faery lady.' She looked Cathy over critically. 'I must say, though, that new way of taking your hair up like that makes the dress look even better than I hoped.'

Nick was there with a thin blonde girl hanging on his arm. Cathy spoke to him, but realised with a shock that her old feeling for him had gone completely, as though it had never been.

Tom Gibbon was there too, holes in the toes of his trainers and a torn teeshirt with *No One Here Gets Out Alive* on it, which made her feel bad as she remembered. She had not seen Tom since the day she had left Dev. She had avoided him at the Gallery, although he had left messages for her to ring him, not wanting to be reminded of that day.

He put his arm around her and kissed her. 'You cow! You didn't ring me. All I did for you.'

'I'm sorry, Tom, I...' She realised then that he was grinning at her.

'It's all right. I'll forgive anybody anything if they paint like this.' He pointed at the painting of Chris and Dev. 'Now that's a masterpiece. A work of undoubted genius, they will say. A searing exposé of the rock world.'

She laughed. 'Tom, you've had too many glasses of the wine.'

He put his mouth near her ear. 'I bring a flask. I need something stronger at previews than this gut rot. All these critics and celebrities give me the shakes.'

'You're a celebrity yourself!'

She turned away, laughing, and was suddenly staring at Dev.

The laughter died away and her heart started to hammer in her throat. How had he got in? Caleb had promised not to send him an invitation.

Dev had lost weight. He looked gaunt and very thin, his eyes deeper, darker.

'Hello, Cathy. Enjoying yourself?'

She swallowed, unable to speak.

'Thanks for sending an invitation.'

'I thought...you were in the States.'

'We came back for the exhibition. Did you think we'd miss it?' He looked at his own portrait and back at her. 'Is that how we always seemed to you? Made of metal, like silver statues. Remote, cold, unreal?'

Her eyes were suddenly brilliant with tears. 'Sometimes. At a show.' It was difficult to talk clearly.

His glance locked with hers, warmer. 'Chris didn't tell me it was a joint portrait, that you'd painted me as well. I thought you had only painted him. I remember that, of course.'

She looked away, stricken, remembering that ghastly afternoon.

He said, gently, 'The pastels of the baby are beautiful, Cathy. Why didn't you show me?'

'Dev, are you all right? You and Paul?'

'We're all right. Not that you care. You don't bother to come down to see him. You never even phone.'

She couldn't let it pass. 'Yes I do. I speak to Mrs. Kaye every morning.'

His eyes blazed. 'You're a liar! What are you giving me? She never said anything to me.'

'Why should she? I asked her not to.'

He was furious. 'Couldn't *I* tell you? Do you have to go behind my back and ask the help?'

She said, simply, 'I didn't think you'd want to talk to me. You've never telephoned. I didn't want to bother you either. I know you're always busy. I thought it would be easier.'

'Easier for *who*, Cathy?'

'Easier for both of us.'

'And what about *me*, Cathy? What makes it easier for *me?*' Chris was there, next to Dev, shoulder to shoulder, the bones of his face standing out. 'You could have spoken to me for a few minutes.'

'We haven't got anything to say to each other, Chris. You've got your friend back. That's what you worked for. That's what you wanted, isn't it? *I'm* the one on the outside now.'

She turned and walked away, her legs trembling.

The exhibition was a huge critical and financial success. All the paintings were sold, the big Easy Connection painting going to the Tate's collection of contemporary painting, and Cathy had enough commissions to keep her busy for years. Even the critics, who had come prepared to damn the exhibition, deeply suspicious of a celebrity's wife, found themselves writing eulogistic reviews. For the public, Cathy was the youngest and most fashionable find. Not since David Hockney, had the art world found such a glamorous, romantic figure allied to great talent. The spotlight of publicity swung on to her once again.

But this time, Cathy hardly noticed. She had become practically a recluse, in the small flat high above the city streets, only emerging to buy food and art materials. She was shut into a personal agony. Seeing Dev and Chris at the Private View had awoken all the feelings she had tried to bury, feelings she had refused to recognise. Now, when she thought it was too late and nothing could be changed or altered, they surfaced with increased intensity. She longed to hear the sound of Dev's voice. She dreamed about him at night, and woke, aching with physical desire.

She locked the door, took the phone off the hook and began to paint for her next exhibition, beginning with a second portrait of Janey Adams. This time she would paint Janey Adams, the woman, not the goddess.

She saw, from an old copy of the *NME*, wrapped around her lettuce in the street market, that half the dates in the big Easy Connection US tour had been cancelled owing to overwork and illness in the band. She stood in the street staring down at the paper, her hands shaking. There was a full-page picture of Dev and Chris leaning moodily against a whitewashed brick wall either side of a prison-like window.

The stall holder looked at it over her shoulder and snorted.

'Overwork? I should be so lucky! Too much booze and dope more likely. Too stoned to climb on the stage.'

A few weeks later her radio told her that police had seized a quantity of drugs from Easy Connection's hotel suite in Stockholm.

Chapter Seventeen

The leaves fell from the plane trees and the winter days drew in.

'You were right,' Cathy told Janey, abruptly. 'Now I know you better I realise I only painted the superstar. This is going to be a much better portrait.'

It was nearly finished. Janey was sitting the way she had sat dozens of times in Cathy's room, half-lying, one leg tucked under her, her arms stretched out along the back of the sofa, staring straight ahead into the gas fire, her face full of moving shadows in the darkening afternoon. A woman in the shadows, very sensual, waiting.

But this afternoon Janey could not relax at all. She was increasingly tense.

'I don't know what's the matter with me. I feel terrible. Restless, apprehensive. I feel something is going to happen. I'm sorry, Cathy, I can't keep still today. I won't stay. I think I ought to be somewhere else. Do you mind if I ring my studio?'

'Maybe you need a holiday,' Cathy said, concerned, picking up the phone and putting its receiver back on the rest. She held it out to Janey and it began to ring furiously. They both laughed.

'It's a new *life* I need,' Janey said, sighing. 'Not a holiday.'

'It's your manager, Janey.'

'Why would he be ringing here? He knows I don't like...' She took the telephone. 'Well, what do you want now?'

She listened and Cathy watching, saw the sudden greenish pallor spread over her face. She put the phone down and turned from it looking like a sleepwalker, her eyes blank.

'It's not true,' she said. Her voice was hoarse and cracked. 'I know it's not true...It *can't* be...'

Cathy felt her heart beating unpleasantly. 'Janey, what's happened? Tell me. What's not true?'

'It's Jay. He's crashed his car on the motorway. Coming down from Glasgow. They say he's dead. Three of them are dead. The Bird Lovers. But it's n-not true...It can't be true...'

She swayed and her legs began to buckle under her. Cathy caught her and thrust a chair behind her knees. She pushed her head down, and after a moment, Janey began to shake and cry. Cathy bent to help, then straightened slowly, staring down at Janey. Quickly, her mind made up, she went to the telephone, dialled a number and spoke to two other people before she finally got the person she wanted.

'Dave, can you come over quickly? Janey's here and she needs you badly. Jay's dead.'

Jay's funeral, with two other members of his band, four days later, was attended by half the rock world of London. Janey stood between Dave Hampton and Ronnie Craig, dramatic in a long black coat, looking straight ahead, thinking of Jay's brilliant green eyes smiling at her.

'Come for a swim, baby?' She could almost hear his voice. She was unaware of the tears running down her cheeks, mingling with the cold rain.

Cathy carefully clipped the photograph from the evening newspaper. Although it was blurry, she knew just how Janey had looked. She had been standing nearby at the funeral, her eyes fixed on Janey so as not to see the coffin being lowered into the dark, soaked trench.

One day she would paint another portrait of Janey and complete the triptych. She had Jane Adams, the great star, the goddess, and Janey Adams, the woman, the life force. Now she needed Jane Adams, the mourning woman, *Death.*

Death.

Cathy was haunted by Jay's death. He had been so young, so burningly alive. She kept remembering him, as he had been at the awards reception, poised in the doorway, thin and tall, with his silver-gilt hair and blazing green eyes, full of wild laughter. She painted a portrait of him, working from the drawings she had made after the reception, and remembered, with a chill of fear, her conviction that Jay had to be drawn quickly, before any of the others, because something might happen to him.

Jay was in the dark leather clothes he had worn that night. Somewhere in the background was a faint greenish glow, illuminating his pale hair and skin, adding depth and glitter to the green eyes. In the dark background was the mysterious silhouette of a girl. Jay was waiting too, poised, dangerous, waiting maybe for the girl in the background, because he was half-turned towards her in the deeper shadows, but he was not looking at her. He didn't need to. He had only to lift a hand and she would come.

Two weeks after the funeral, Janey came into Cathy's studio. She looked pale but calm, in a dark suit and a grey high-necked sweater. She was carrying an overnight bag.

'I came to say goodbye for a while. I'm going to Italy to study.'

Cathy tried to smile, glad that Jay's portrait was turned to the wall. 'You're really going at last then?'

'I'm not wasting any more time. I knew I'd made a terrible mistake, marrying Jay, but now I have a second chance and I'm not messing it up again. I may not be *free*, Cathy, but at least I'm in charge of my own life now.'

Cathy said, slowly, 'What about Dave?'

Janey smiled. 'It's all right. He thinks I ought to go too. It's all right between us now. That's another reason I came. To thank you. I would never have telephoned him. And neither would he.'

'I know.'

Janey looked at her. 'You didn't fall for him?'

'A bit maybe. But it was no good. We found that out.'

'We'll probably get married when I feel better about Jay. But now I just want some time to be myself. That's another thing I have to thank you for. Just seeing you reminded me that once I had high ambitions, and I was accepting second best. I feel I've wasted so much time. I've cancelled all my rock engagements, and I've got terrible cold feet, thinking I won't be good enough for Calvi, but I'm going all the same.'

She wandered around the studio, touching objects, not seeing them.

'It was Jay's fault, you know. He was full of dope and driving too fast, Rick said. He was the only one to get out alive, and he's pretty smashed up. Jay swore to me last time he was off it for ever. If only...It's the waste, Cathy...*life.*' She brushed her hand over her cheeks. 'Oh well. I have to go now. A radio interview at the BBC before the plane. I'm going to miss you. But I'll be back quite often to see you and Dave.'

Cathy said, going to the door with her, smiling, 'Send me a picture postcard. I've always wanted to see Italy.'

Janey said, suddenly excited, 'Cathy, come for a visit. A long time. There's an extra room in the flat I'm renting.'

Cathy was frightened. 'I don't think I could. I mean, I couldn't go just now. There are paintings I've got to do...'

'Later then. Let me know. We'll have a great time.'

The smiled at each other and Cathy realised suddenly how much she would miss Janey. She put out her hands. 'You're going to be a great opera singer. I don't know why I'm crying.'

Janey hugged her. 'You're my best friend, Cathy. You've helped me more than you know.'

'And you've helped me. Helped me to see things.'

Janey looked at Cathy, seriously, hesitating. She took two steps across the landing and then turned back. She said abruptly, almost blurting it out, 'I saw Dev at Hammersmith last night. Backstage.'

Cathy's stomach muscles clenched painfully. 'With a girl?'

'No, not then. But he looked...like a wild man. Ill. Reckless.'

'He'd been drinking.'

'They all had. Chris was as high as a kite on something. But Dev looked terrible. His eyes...He was desperate, Cathy.

Cathy stared back at her, waiting.

Janey said, with difficulty, 'I've got to say this, even if you never want to talk to me again. Because of what you did for me. And there's no one else to tell you. Cathy, I think you should go back to Dev and the baby. I don't think he can make it alone.'

'What about my painting? *My* life?' Cathy's voice was icy.

Janey took a deep breath. 'If you want to know, I don't think *you* can make it either. You're too cut off in this place, and you're working too hard all the time.' She looked around at Cathy's latest work propped against the walls. 'These paintings – they're very beautiful, but they're so cold and strange they make me shiver. They are superhuman somehow. You are losing touch with us humans. I can't see the love and understanding that used to be in your paintings. You're becoming kind of unearthly. You need someone to keep hold of you, before you float away completely.'

Cathy, ashen, went on staring at her.

'And there's another thing. I think you're in love with Dev. Maybe you don't know. Go back, Cathy. You need somebody. We all need somebody. A *friend*. Someone to face the darkness with.'

She waited but Cathy was silent. 'Dev can't take you over now. You're a free person. I'm sorry. I had to say it. I know it's not my business.'

She walked away down the stairs. On the landing below, she paused and looked up at Cathy, flicking her heavy hair back over her shoulders. She was smiling.

'I just thought of something. You know Kris Kristofferson's song, *Me and Bobby McGee?* *'Freedom's just another word for nothing left to lose.'*

Chapter Eighteen

Cathy worked. She worked harder than ever, trying to shut out the sound of Janey's words.

A card came from Italy and a letter, but she put them behind the clock and forgot them. She buried herself in work, painting hour after hour until she could no longer see the canvas.

She painted the people at the supermarket checkout, waiting with their baskets. The bright packaging colours and shining chrome and plastic, framed faces broken with tiredness, fear, greed, boredom.

She painted the people on the underground, featureless in the strange, unreal light, against the dead grey paint.

She painted people moving along the road, zombie-like, reflecting in glass shop fronts, ghosts lost in dark space.

And looking at them, she saw with horror that Janey had been right. These people were specimens, moving in a surreal dream. They were all doomed and waiting. Alone. People facing the darkness. And the bottom of Cathy's stomach seemed to drop away when she realised what they were waiting for. Death and annihilation.

They were not the kind of paintings she had wanted to paint for people. She had hoped to paint pictures that were life-giving, showing the beauty and importance of life. These paintings had an eerie beauty, but they were cold, without hope. There seemed nothing she could do about it. The deadness, the coldness and despair, were heavy inside her.

Desperately she turned to the final portrait of Janey. A single figure, straight and slender, mourning, in her dark clothes. But she too was lost in the weaving shadows of death. The bones of her face were shining ivory, the eyes deep and terrible with loss.

Death. The ultimate freedom. Nothing left to lose.

Dave Hampton, passing through London from a successful tour of the States, on his way to Italy and Janey, called in to see her. He stared at the portrait of Jay, looking shaken.

'That's Janey in the background, isn't it? How did you know Jay was like that? That's just how he was. A kind of seductive wizard. A witch-man feeding on girls and sex. Feeding on Janey. They say he was into black magic. He had a hold on her.'

'She said he saved her life.'

'It was more than that. They met when we were just getting started, and after that he always had a part of her. I couldn't do anything, and Janey wouldn't admit it.'

Cathy said, 'He's dead. All that energy and freedom. *Dead.*'

He looked away from the painting directly at Cathy. 'I hated him. I'm glad he's dead. She would never have got away if he'd lived. I don't know why anybody should bother about him.'

Cathy's painting got darker, obsessive. She began to make paintings of shadowy figures groping in a dark mist, their faces disembodied, like polished ivory or glittering steel, skull-like, hands clutching fluttering rags. The portrait commissions were left, forgotten. She went on painting helplessly, despairingly, because it was the only thing she could do.

The big canvases packed the room. To make more space she moved her divan into the small back kitchen and slept among the saucepans and unwashed plates. The largest canvas, five metres by three, was too large for an easel. She hammered nails into a retaining rail on the wall to hold it firmly as she painted, and the huge picture spread its darkness along the length of the room, intense and dominating.

The figures had started to disintegrate now, the planes of the faces breaking up, the eyes dissolving and slipping jelly-like, the mouths open and screaming, the bodies shredding into skin, fluttering like the rags in the blowing dark dust. And in the dust were old hands, clutching child hands half-skeleton.

In December, Caleb Crow came stamping up the stairs crossly, on one of his rare visits. He paused for breath on the half-landing below and looked up at her. His mouth was very red in his deep beard.

'My god, what a place to live. Where are the golden eagles?'

Cathy leaned over the banisters, smiling, 'Are you going to make it?'

'Mahomet comes to the mountain. Your phone's not working *again*. What's wrong?'

'I don't know.' She went back into the room and looked for the phone. It was on the floor in a corner, jammed between two paintings, which had knocked the receiver off its hook.

'I'm sorry,' she said, guiltily, 'I didn't know...'

'You're cut off up here like a bloody Trappist nun. *Are* there Trappist...' Caleb's rich, cultured voice stopped abruptly. He was halted on the threshold, staring at the crowding paintings. He came slowly into the room and sat down rather heavily on the tea chest she used as a stool. He looked grey.

Cathy said, alarmed, 'Are you all right?'

'*All right?* No, I am not *all right*. Not *all right* at all.' He went on staring around the room. 'How long?'

Cathy shrugged and avoided his eyes. 'Do you want tea or anything? I haven't got any beer.'

He ignored her, got up again and started moving around the room, pulling out canvases, his hawk's eyes reading the surfaces. Silent. His shoulders sagged, his head sank forward like an old man.

Cathy sat on the window sill, huddled, watching him. The silence lengthened. She said at last, desperately, 'What do you think?'

Caleb turned to her. For the first time she had known him there was no humour in his dark eyes. They were grim and deadly serious.

'Horrifying. Perhaps the most terrifying paintings I've seen in my lifetime.'

Cathy's eyes filled with tears. 'I can't stop. I hate them.'

'Bloody masterpieces, of course. Goya, Dore, Bacon. Especially that.' He pointed to the biggest. *'The Lost? After the Terror? After the Bomb?'*

She swallowed and looked away.

'How? Where?'

Her voice was muffled. 'I dream...but I'm not asleep. In the day. I have these...visions.'

She stood up jerkily. 'Caleb, I can't stand it. I think they're pictures of the future. Like second-sight. They keep coming.'

Her luminous grey-violet eyes looked at him, frightened and desperate. *'What am I going to do?'*

He went on staring at the huge painting, appalled at the pain and intensity. He said, soberly, 'I don't know, Cathy.'

'I'll go mad. All I think about is death. Am I mad already?'

'Does it feel like madness?'

'No.' Her voice was bleak. 'It feels like the truth. Like the future. There're going to be terrible bombs, terrible events, and we're all going to die. It'll be like that.'

'We have to show them. January. I'll cancel John Ebury.'

'I don't think...'

'Oh yes. Might make our mad masters think again. These paintings – perhaps they are a warning. Have you thought of that? A *warning* only?'

Cathy shook her head despairingly. 'How do I know? Caleb, please help me. I can't bear to paint any more of them. *I can't.* But I can't seem to do anything else. And what's it all for anyway? Why should I bother when it's all going to be destroyed?'

'I ought to tell you to go on. You'd end up in the funny house – but what's that against a few more paintings like these? There's always a price. Vincent paid it. Richard Dadd paid it. Countless poets. But I've got fond of you, dammit, and I don't fancy trekking up to Friern, so we'll have to do something.'

Cathy gave a choked laugh. 'You're incredible, Caleb. I think you'd have us all in batteries, de-beaked and de-clawed, like chickens, if we laid masterpieces.'

'I certainly would. What are artists good for except to make art? But after all, I've got my investment to protect.' The ironical humour was back in his eyes. 'So I'll fix up a holiday for you. You've been overworking. My God, I never thought I'd hear myself saying that to one of my contract artists! The States. You can do some promotion work while you're there.'

'No – not the States,' Cathy said, quickly. Dev was often in the States. She didn't want to meet him by chance.

'And you'll have to get out of this place. It's no good for you. Too cut off. Ivory tower. Mount Delphi. You'll be handing out prophecies if you stay here. There's a studio in a community block down in Hackney. An old warehouse. Painters. Craftspeople. People around when the going gets rough.'

'What's the good of that if I go on painting these things?' She was suddenly frightened, not at all sure she wanted to leave the flat to face people again.

'Have you painted anything else recently? Anything at all?'

'No.'

'What's this, then?'

He had been rootling through the stacked paintings and come up with a small canvas. Cathy looked at it, puzzled. 'I don't remember.'

It was a small picture of brilliant multicolour and golden light. In the radiance there was the suggestion of small figures climbing up, amid flowers and leaves in a spiral form.

Caleb looked at it thoughtfully. 'It's a lingam shape. Like an oval stone egg. That mean anything to you?'

Cathy stared at him, and went pale. An oval stone – like the Atlantis pendant which Dev wore, the wishing stone he was so superstitious about.

She remembered the painting now. She had been very tired, playing about with the pleasant colours, not painting seriously, trying to stop the dark visions coming. Now she looked at the canvas again and saw that the chance colours had formed themselves into a rough oval with a cloudy surface, which the eye could see as figures and flowers. It really looked like Dev's oval pendant, with its small, carved figures. A subconscious memory?

'It's not finished.'

She shook her head wearily, not bothering to answer.

'There's your way out. Oppose the death wish.' Caleb said, obscurely, and stamped off.

After he had gone Cathy stood for a long time looking at the small painting.

Caleb was a very clever man. Perhaps she would try to work on it. She put the canvas on her easel and began to paint out some blank areas with a soft pale pink.

Four hours later she was still painting. The canvas shone with brilliant light. A kind of paradise. No dark tones. No horrors. Peace, happiness, beauty, banishing death.

Exhausted, Cathy dropped on to her divan without undressing and slept deeply for the first time in weeks.

She dreamed of Dev. He was holding the Atlantis Stone, but his hand was shaking and he looked ill and crazy. Then the dream split and Chris was there, moving, whirling, there was confusion and shouting, and an alarm bell, ringing on and on, growing in urgency.

Chapter Nineteen

She came awake, her heart pounding and fearful.
Something was terribly wrong.
The knowledge was there, clear and sure. Something had happened to Dev. And Chris too, maybe. Something bad. She must go to them right away. She got up quickly, swaying dizzily, panic stricken. *Death was everywhere.* She breathed deeply and tried to get a hold on herself, trying to think.

Where should she go? She did not know where they were. Maybe not even in England. And what could she say or do when she got there? She would look so stupid if she was wrong and they would be so cruel, getting their own back. She could imagine the scene. Dev and Chris lounging on a sofa, watching her maliciously, enjoying her embarrassment.

'Our little baby's back, Dev.'
'Mother love, Chris.'
'Worried about us, Dev.'
'*Dreaming* about us, Chris.'
'Did we have our clothes on, Cathy?' They would look at each other and laugh.

A sudden wave of longing for them swept over her, leaving her as shaken physically as the dream itself. She wanted to see them so much. To hug Dev close and feel his body warm and strong. If Dev had been killed...

Cathy took a deep breath as the pain hit her. She went to the sink and drank a glass of water, her hands shaking so much it spilled on the floor.

It was just a dream, after all. She would look such a *fool.* But she could still hear in her head the sound of the alarm bell ringing on insistently. Suddenly she didn't care if she made a fool of herself. It was late, nearly twelve o'clock, but somebody must still be up.

She went into the studio, re-lit the gas fire and picked the telephone off the floor.

There was no reply from Dev's London flat. The telephone rang again and again. But Mrs. Kaye came to the phone quickly at Cox's Farm. No, Dev wasn't there. He was off abroad somewhere. Concerts in Germany or Spain. She didn't know for sure when he would be back. Yes, the baby was fine. Was anything wrong? Dev would be so glad to hear from her. He hadn't been himself for a long time...Couldn't she come down and just talk to him?

Cathy, feeling even more stupid, phoned a number Bill Hopkins had given her long ago. An irritated voice questioned her and refused to put her through, even though the desperation in her voice was obvious. She would have to leave her number and they might contact her again.

It was nearly an hour later that Bill Hopkins himself came on the line from Germany. He sounded cold and angry.

'Dev's in Barcelona. Why do you want to speak to him? Hasn't he suffered enough without you trying to rake it all up again?'

'I don't want to talk to him,' Cathy said, desperately. 'But there's something wrong. Are you *sure* he's all right? Couldn't you speak to Chris or someone? Please, I know you hate me and blame me for leaving, but just phone Chris. There's something wrong, Bill, honestly. What harm can it do?'

Bill Hopkins sounded weary. 'I don't blame you, Cathy. I know Dev's difficult, but he's had a very bad time. It's hard watching a man breaking up. I just hoped you'd stay a bit longer. All right. I'll get hold of Chris.'

'Thanks.'

He rang back almost immediately, his voice tense, worried. 'Dev isn't there. Chris isn't there. No one knows where either of them are.'

Cathy's heart was beating irregularly. 'But the concerts...'

'They did the two gigs here in Germany. They were having a few days off before the big concert in Barcelona. Nobody knows what actually happened. They all thought he was somewhere else.'

'Chris?'

'Took off earlier this evening in a chartered jet. No one knows where or why. Gregg Fisher has disappeared too. You're right. There's trouble. I'm flying back.'

Cathy put the duvet round her shoulders and sat in front of the fire shivering and frightened, waiting.

She had dropped into a light sleep, dream laden with the ringing of emergency alarm bells, when the sound merged into the urgent ringing of her own door bell.

Her heart had started to bang unpleasantly. She looked at the clock. It was nearly three o'clock.

'Who is it,' she said, into the entryphone, her voice cracking.

'Chris.'

Chris. Her stomach somersaulted with fear. What had happened to Dev? She pressed the door release with shaky fingers and in seconds he was running up the stairs. He was pale, dishevelled, needing a shave. He pushed her back into the room and snapped on the main light.

'Quick, get a coat. It's Dev. I'll take you to the hospital. He's taken an overdose of smack.'

So the newspaper report was true. She stood momentarily paralysed, remembering Janey Adams singing *St. James Infirmary,* the tears running down her cheeks.

'What can I do?'

'It's usually fatal, but you might get him out of the coma.'

When she did not move he gripped her shoulders, his face twisted with fury. 'Listen, you selfish little bitch. He's *dying*. Do you understand? *Dying!* He's not hooked. He took an overdose to kill himself. Got that?'

'It can't be true,' she stammered. 'He wouldn't. It must have been a mistake. They say it's easy to overdose.'

'No mistake,' said Chris, bitterly. 'He had it all planned. Said he was going to Paris, but flew home instead. I was in Barcelona, but I suddenly had a crazy hunch. I *knew*. I had to charter a flight to get back to London quick, and we found him in the flat. He was still alive, but he wanted to die all right. And it's *your* fault.'

The slashing pain made her gasp aloud. 'No!'

'He wanted to die. He's been in hell. He fell apart when you left him.'

'I don't believe you. He had the baby. All those girls. And he never came near. Never phoned once. He didn't want me.'

'For God's sake, Cathy, when are you going to grow up? He's in love with you. You don't turn it on and off. He did everything he could to make you love him, looked after you, gave you presents, even tried to make you jealous, but you couldn't be bothered. You just – walked away. You didn't even care for me. All you care about is your painting. No human being can get near you.'

Cathy shuddered and involuntarily her eyes went to her painting on the wall. Chris looked where she was looking, and then swiftly round the room. He recoiled visibly. 'Christ Almighty.'

Cathy said, wildly, 'I never pretended. I *told* him. He knew. You knew. I won't be blamed for Dev. It's not my fault. It must have been a mistake.'

'Do you know what day it was yesterday?'

'*Day?* Do you mean the date? Tuesday? Or maybe it was Wednesday, the...'

'Day!' he said, savagely. 'You see how much it meant to you? Yesterday was your *wedding anniversary. Now* will you come to the hospital?'

Chris drove to the hospital swiftly. Despite her thick jeans and sweater and quilted jacket, Cathy could not stop shivering. They did not speak. She knew Chris would never forgive her, because he would never forgive himself.

At the hospital an official hurried them to a lift through the small knot of waiting pressmen and photographers, who woke up enough to take a few shots of them.

'Hey, Chris, what's the latest?'

'Is he gonna make it?'

Chris shrugged and shook his head, but did not stop to talk to them. He put his arm around Cathy's shoulders and hurried her past.

'Who's the girl?'

'Catherine Harlow, the painter.'

'Cathy Devlin, Dev's wife.'

'I thought the marriage broke up.'

The lift carried them up high to a corridor of private wards.

'Wait in here,' said a nurse. 'The doctors are still with him.'

The small waiting room was empty. It had a wall bench, a narrow window looking down into a small yard and a dozen old magazines.

Chris swore and dropped on to the bench wearily. 'I don't know how the press got wind of it. I tried to keep it quiet.'

'It's not your fault.'

He picked up a copy of *Horse and Hound,* flipped through half the pages and threw it down, disgusted. 'Bloody hell!'

Suddenly time seemed to have stopped. There was no sound at all out in the corridor and no movement. Silence. After the hurry and panic, a time warp.

Cathy stood by fhe window looking down, but it was dark and all she could see was Chris' reflection. He was leaning forward, his elbows on his knees, staring at the floor. It hurt her to see him looking so ill and defeated. She wished she could go and put her arms around him for comfort. Impossible.

She rested her forehead against the window. 'What are we going to do if he dies, Chris?'

He did not reply.

'At least you got him here.'

'We couldn't get in at first, Gregg and I. He'd locked and barricaded the front door. I had to climb across from the next balcony and break the window.'

Cathy felt sick. The flat was on the seventh floor and the balconies far apart, with only narrow ledges between them. Chris must have been demented to have considered it even.

'You were crazy! You could have fallen.'

'Yeah, crazy. Crazy with guilt.' He closed his eyes. Then suddenly he was looking at her again, direct, searchingly. 'You knew too, didn't you? You were already dressed and waiting when I got to you.'

She looked away. 'Yes, I knew.'

'And did nothing?' His voice was incredulous.

'I didn't know where he was,' Cathy said, in agony. 'I phoned around. The Farm. And I got Bill Hopkins in Germany. I wanted him to find you, but you'd already gone. Bill's flying back.'

'Thank God.' He leaned his head back against the wall. 'We'll need Bill to get us out of this one. The story out, another bloody drugs charge...' He stopped. 'If he lives.'

Cathy said, 'I phoned the flat, but there was no reply.' A sudden thought struck her and she went very pale. 'Chris, he must have been there all the time listening to the phone ringing. *Dying.*'

Chris looked at her. 'Knowing it was you.'

Cathy turned away quickly. Chris got up and moved about the room restlessly. He said, abruptly, 'Cathy, those paintings you're doing...'

She wiped the tears away with her arm. 'Don't say a thing.'

'Get out of that place. You'll have a breakdown.'

'Mind your own business. You're not running my life as well as Dev's.'

He was furious. 'I don't run Dev.'

'You could have fooled me. All right – my paintings are the most important thing to me. That's all I am – just my paintings and they take over. I can't help it. But I do care about people. You have no right to say...'

She brushed the tears off her cheeks again, angrily.

'Because I'm a woman I've no right to be obsessed or serious about work. I'm supposed to think of it as a kind of hobby until the real stuff comes along – a baby, a man. Then I can go on doing it, provided it takes second place. But it's okay for your music to come first.'

He stuffed his hands in the zip pockets of his short leather jacket and stood looking at her. 'I'd give it up tomorrow, Cathy. For you. Or for Dev. That's the difference between us.'

She stared at him, her heart twisting. 'I don't believe you.'

He shrugged and sat down again, grey with fatigue.

Cathy stood in the centre of the room, her panic rising. 'Why don't they tell us what's happening?' She looked out into the corridor, but it was deserted, the shaded light making a pool of brightness on the empty nurses' desk at the end of the corridor. She shut the door. 'I don't know why I'm here. I can't do anything. I can't change anything. Why did you bring me? Dev doesn't want me.'

Chris laughed.

'Charis. Tara Linstrom.'

'Don't make excuses, Cathy. What you really mean is you don't want Dev. Or me. You've never forgiven us for that night at the Farm.'

Cathy turned to the window and looked out at the darkness.

Chris said, wearily. 'You go on blaming Dev, but you've got it wrong, Cathy. That day – *I* found you, so you were my girl. *I* kept you at the Farm. You were there to keep me warm. Dev didn't need a girl. Charis had followed him from L.A.

'You know Dev was crazy about her. But she was just a rich wild lady out for kicks. She took everything, got bored and took off. But Dev couldn't get over her. He doesn't go in for superficial relationships. We hadn't seen her for a while, then, the day we left the States, she turned up at the hotel and begged him to take her back. Big reconciliation scene and she's on our plane back to London.'

Cathy stared at him. *'Reconciliation?* I don't understand. Why did he make me stay then? Why did he make me have sex?'

'*I* made you stay. But then Dev wanted you so much I handed you over.'

'No, that's not true. You and Dev made a deal. He told me. Dev had something you wanted.'

The colour deepened under his cheekbones. 'Okay. When you found out we were Easy Connection you were ready to run. I knew you weren't about to climb into anybody's bed. So when Dev offered, I traded.'

Cathy said, insistently, 'What did you 'trade' me for Chris? What did you want so much?'

'Charis.'

'Charis!'

'Dev had had her for two years. She was just the most important thing in his whole life. He traded *her* to get *you.*'

Cathy stared at him dumbly. 'Y-you loved her too?'

He smiled, and Cathy felt a shiver run up her back. 'Let's say I wanted her. For revenge. She made Dev crawl, Cathy, sexual humiliation. In front of us. Turned him into a neurotic mess. Nearly broke up the band. She's a dog, Cathy. The lowest. I had to stand by and watch.'

Cathy heard the agony in his voice. 'And I swore to myself that one day I would put her through what she was putting Dev through.'

The silence extended itself. 'I got what I wanted. I always do. But I didn't know how much it would cost. *You.*' There was another silence. 'It wasn't worth it. You've never been unimportant to either of us, Cathy.'

'Chris,' Cathy said, suddenly, watching him, *'has* Dev got another lady, here in town?'

He hesitated.

'It's too late. Tell me the truth.'

'He's on his own.'

'Those girls he brought to the Farm, Jilly and something?'

'Pick-ups to make you jealous.'

'Tara Linstrom?'

'Media promotion. Dev got her into the papers.'

'Australia. The Far East tour. You said he lived it up. He was with Charis?'

He shook his head. 'He didn't touch her. It was my turn.' He smiled. 'It was...interesting.'

Cathy shivered again. 'It was all lies.'

He leapt to his feet and paced the small room uncontrollably.

'Look, I know I'm responsible for putting him here. You and me together.'

'What did you tell him about me?'

Chris paused and confronted her, his eyes fierce and accusing. 'I told him you were seeing Dave Hampton. And that wasn't a lie. I saw you myself, holding hands at the Venue.'

Cathy flushed. 'You knew it was nothing. I thought Dev was your friend. How could you do that to him?'

'My best friend. But I wanted you. I told you not to trust me. I told him I'd take you off him if I could. It was easy to start up all those quarrels. You were so full of hate and resentment. There's no law says you've got to give your best friend the woman you love and walk away.'

'But Chris, what about me – *my* happiness? If you really loved me, you'd want to make me happy. You think a broken marriage is a good way to make me happy?'

'You'd be happier with me.'

He sounded arrogant and sulky, like a child. Cathy said, sadly, 'You know neither of us could be happy if it made Dev miserable. You've said it already – crazy with guilt.'

Chris' light eyes were too bright, staring deeply into hers. She felt very close to him. His mouth was pressed together holding the pain inside. She took and held his hand, wanting to put her arms around him, wanting to kiss away the pain. She looked back into his eyes, letting him read the truth, and heard his indrawn breath.

'You love me, Cathy. You're in love with both of us.'

Cathy said, 'So are you. And Dev.'

He pulled his hand away violently and took a step back. 'Christ, what a bloody mess. I told you – it's Karma. It must be Karma. What the hell are we going to do?' He sounded hysterical, horrified.

Cathy went back to the window.

There was a faint light in the sky. She looked at her watch. It was past four o'clock. She remembered something about souls slipping away with the darkness and could not stop shaking. She tried to concentrate her energies, to help Dev lying nearby. Was his spirit drifting away?

'I thought I hated him. But after the baby came I felt so different. I wanted to tell him, but he was icy. I couldn't get near him.'

'He was waiting for you to make the first move.'

'I did try, but I was shy. I kept seeing him as a great rock star. And you told me he'd been living it up on tour. Then there was that trouble with you. And those girls. He promised never to bring girls like that to the house, so it seemed like just another way of telling me it was all over. I thought I'd better get out and get it over with quickly, and then we could all start again.'

'I never thought you'd walk out. I thought you'd turn to me. But you wouldn't see me either. I lost you too. It's been bad, Cathy.'

'For me too.'

'I tried to phone, explain, but you wouldn't talk to me.'

'I thought we should all start again. I thought if I worked hard enough...But the loving didn't stop. It got worse. Chris, if he dies...Oh what are they doing? Why doesn't someone come?'

She flung open the door again, and saw two white-coated doctors and a nurse coming out of the next room. They stopped to confer, serious, talking low, looking very grim. The nurse walked away with one of the doctors down the corridor. The other turned to Cathy.

She said, faintly, 'Chris, I think he's...Chris!'

'All right.' He pushed past and the doctor began to talk to him quickly, smiling.

Smiling.

Her jelly legs carried her forward.

'...a very narrow squeak indeed. He's weak, but he's okay. If you'd got to him half an hour later it would have been too late. Young lady, you look on the point of collapse yourself. I take it you're the Cathy he keeps asking for.'

Cathy smiled, blinking away tears. 'I'm okay. Can I go in?'

'For a few minutes. Don't get him too excited. I'll be back when I've spoken to the reporters. Good news for the fans!'

He went away down the corridor. Cathy hesitated and looked at Chris. He was chalk white.

'You saved his life, Chris.'

He stared at her. The hostility had gone. There was only bone tiredness. 'Twice. Getting him here in time and telling you the truth.'

She looked at him, still hesitating. 'I love you, Chris, but not as much as Dev.'

'Okay. I knew you'd find out sooner or later. Go in Cathy. I'll wait.'

'I won't be long.'

'Won't you, Cathy?' He sounded defeated. He sat down on the corridor floor, his head tilted back against the wall, his eyes closed. Cathy's heart wrenched with love and pity. She put her hand against his cheek. He turned his head and kissed her fingers. Then, after a moment, he smiled at her. 'Go in, Cathy. He's alive.'

Chapter Twenty

Dev did not hear the door open and close again. He was laying on his back, still, his eyes closed. His skin was drained to a curious bluish pallor, and his long fair hair was spread out on the pillow. For a heart-stopped moment Cathy thought that he was dead, then she realised that his lips were moving. He was *swearing*, a long string of vivid obscenities.

She brushed the tears away, wanting to laugh hysterically. People weren't supposed to swear on their death beds.

'*Dev.*'

His eyes blinked open, intense, eager, and then the eagerness faded. He put his arm across his eyes.

'What a bloody cock-up. I should have gone to a hotel. It must have been Chris and his effing ESP. I'll kill the interfering sod.'

'Shut up. He saved your life. You ought to be thanking him.'

He laughed, his voice cracking hoarsely in the middle.'

'What's the matter with your throat?'

'They pumped my stomach out.'

Cathy swallowed. She went slowly across the room and stood by his bed. 'How are you?'

'Why did you come, Cathy?'

'I don't know.'

He turned his head away. 'Listen, I'll give you a divorce if you want to marry Chris. But not Dave Hampton. He's too hung up on Janey Adams.'

'I don't *want...*'

'I love you so much, Cathy. I want you to be happy. I suppose I always knew you'd never be able to love me after what I did, but I couldn't give you up until I'd tried. When you walked out, I knew it was all over.'

'I want to come back,' Cathy said.

His head jerked around. He sat up violently, staring at her.

'I'll kill him. I'll fucking murder him. Chris made you come. What did he do – use a shotgun?'

Cathy said evenly, looking at him directly, 'Nobody makes me do anything I don't want to do now, Dev. I'm free and I can choose. I can earn enough to keep myself. I can walk away if I want to.'

'Why then? Because of the baby?'

'No.'

Dev leaned back, wearily. 'What do you want with me, Cathy?'

'I think I need you. Not to look after me. I can look after myself. But I need you all the same. Janey Adams said, *someone to face the darkness with.* A friend. I thought perhaps you might need that too. Your paintings. I didn't understand them at first. I thought the hand shape reaching was *you,* but that's not true. The fire, the light, the *changing,* is you. The reaching hand shape is what you're looking for. A hand held out in the darkness. Tonight, when I thought I wouldn't see you again *ever...*'

'Pity isn't enough for me, Cathy.'

Cathy laughed shortly. '*Pity?* Dev, you're a world famous rock star. A millionaire with a country house, a London apartment and three cars. You've got a great creative talent. Thousands of people all over the world idolise you and would die for you. *Pity?* You're raving.'

'It's a shame none of it means anything to me any more.' He closed his eyes. 'The only thing I want, I can't have.'

'In case you've forgotten, you're a father too. What about your son? He loves you. You had *no right...*'

She realised then how weak Dev was. Tears had forced their way under his closed lids and were shining on his lashes. She took a deep breath and looked at the floor. 'I don't pity you, Dev. I love you.'

There was a silence. When she looked at him at last, Dev's eyes were wide open, staring at her. 'It's a bit sudden, isn't it, Cathy?'

Colour burned in her cheeks, but she did not look away, letting him read the truth for himself. 'I love the way your hair grows, and your mouth and your long hands, the shape of your shoulders and body, your long thighs. I love the way you move. You make me feel weak, just looking at you. I keep dreaming about you.'

Dev tried to smile, but his voice was shaky. 'Do I have my clothes on, Cathy?'

'I knew you'd say that!'

He laughed and reaching quickly, pulled her to him. She held on to him, tightly, shaking with reaction.

'I thought you were going to die like Jay Bird. That I'd never see you again.' Her voice was muffled against his hair and shoulder. 'I do love you Dev. I was going to tell you when you came back from the Far East tour. But you wouldn't talk to me. I kissed you, Dev. But you didn't even open your eyes.'

Dev said, ruefully, 'I couldn't. It hurt too much. I thought it was a kind of goodbye kiss. When we got back you looked so beautiful, so happy and excited again, I thought you wanted to talk about a divorce. You see, I was always sure that once you'd had the baby you would leave me. I knew you wouldn't stay after what I'd done.'

The tension was suddenly back between them. Cathy sat away from him.

'I must have been mad, crazy drunk to make you have sex like that,' Dev said, violently.

'Why did you do it to me, Dev? *Why?* I've never understood. You didn't think I wanted it really did you?'

Dev leaned back on the pillows and put his arm across his face again, concealing, Cathy thought.

'I have to tell you about Charis, but...it's difficult. I can't talk about it much even now. We were together a long time. At first I loved her, Cathy. I'd never met anyone like her. She was exciting and beautiful. But she was...warped, twisted, too. I didn't know until it was too late. She obsessed me, like a drug. She didn't love me. But she liked to...play games with me. She enjoyed debasing people, making them crawl. I don't know why – something in her past, maybe. She would...I can't tell you, Cathy. You couldn't *imagine*...'

She saw the tendons in his neck tighten as he tried to swallow. She poured a glass of water from the bedside carafe and he drank it painfully.

'Let's just say, I never thought I'd let another human being do what she did to me. When she left me I got sane again. She came back at the end of the American tour and I brought her back to the Farm. I wanted revenge. I wanted to make her pay and pay again. That day, when *we* first met, I was full of hate, rage, and vodka. But you were there, and suddenly I found I didn't care about Charis any more. I just wanted her out of my life for good, and I realised I'd fallen in love with you. Instantly. Completely.

'But you didn't want me either. You tried to push me away. I thought I'd found another Charis, winding me up until I was begging and crazy, so I took my revenge. On you. On Charis. On all women. I made you have sex.

'But you weren't Charis. You were gentle and sweet, crying and trembling, and afterwards I couldn't let you go. We made love properly, and it was – incredible. Like coming out of a filthy cell into a sunlit garden. I swear I didn't know until later how it seemed to you. I didn't know it was the first time and I'd frightened and terrified you.'

'What about Charis?'

He laughed grimly. 'Chris took her over. I almost feel sorry for her now. Chris has got her panting for him. He's good at that. She follows him around waiting for the boot to go in. And it does. He doesn't like her – for what she did to me. Christ, he was rough with her on the Far East tour. Used her like dirt. He even made her...Well, never mind.

'If only you knew how much I regret everything, Cathy. How much I wanted to make it up to you. But you can't wash out violence and evil just by regretting and wishing, and buying a fur coat. It goes on growing like a cancer. The consequences. All the time it grows – resentment, hatred, fear, revenge. It's still going on for us, isn't it? Dave Hampton told me he thought something bad had happened to you in the past and it was giving you a breakdown.'

'It's a chain,' said Cathy. 'From someone to Charis, Charis to you, and then it spread to Chris and then to me, and then I turned it back on you. I was so full of hate and resentment.'

'I don't know how you stop it,' Dev said. 'I've tried, Cathy.'

She said, hesitant, 'I think you have to start forgiving. Once you start forgiving it contains it somehow. The hatred can't grow and make more hatred.'

'Can you forgive me, Cathy?'

'After the baby was born, I felt differently. I forgave you then, maybe. I thought the baby might have come from the loving, not the forcing. I wanted to tell you, but I had hurt you too much by then, hadn't I? You were so cold and angry. I thought it was too late and you had found someone else and it all started up again.'

'I'm so sorry, Cathy. I wanted to be your whole life and I turned into a jailer.'

He said, despairingly, 'What about your painting and your freedom? And our quarrels? You need your freedom. It wouldn't work, Cathy. I won't be a jailer again.'

Cathy said, 'There are different kinds of freedom. I didn't know that.'

'I couldn't take any more of that quarrelling. It nearly killed me.'

'Me too. Chris...' But she could not tell him what Chris had said about making the quarrels.

'Yeah. *Chris.*' The name hung between them. 'What about Chris? He's going crazy not even seeing you. We both are.'

'Dev, Chris and I – we didn't...'

'I know. But you're in love with him all the same. I've always known how you feel about him. Don't you realise there aren't any secrets between us three?'

She looked away, the colour flooding her pale skin, then back at him. 'Yes, all right, I love Chris too, but not as much as I love you, Dev. I don't understand him, and he can't help me. He doesn't understand about the darkness. But you do. The paintings I've been doing...I'm frightened, Dev. I need a hand held out. I think I may always have loved you. Right from the start when I saw you across the stream. Love at first sight. But I didn't know. It was too soon for me to love. And then, the violence ruined everything.'

Dev was suddenly very pale. 'What do you want to do, Cathy?'

'I don't know. I just don't know. I thought it was so difficult walking away, getting my freedom, learning to live alone, becoming a person, but that was the easy part. What is difficult is learning to stay, learning to work it out.

'I'd like to try again. I need you, Dev. I need someone to love me and care if I die. I need someone to face the darkness with. We're maybe going to die soon.'

'Everybody dies, Cathy, sooner or later.'

'I don't want to die alone.'

'Everybody dies alone too. I found that out last night.'

She said, hopelessly, 'It's no good then? I know I'm not offering you anything worth having. I'm always going to be buried in my work. I'd like to try again, but there are so many problems. Work, love, freedom...Chris.'

'Cathy, you want life should come packed in polystyrene blocks like a video player, with all the loose ends tucked in neatly so nothing gets broken or damaged, so we don't even have to feel anything any more? No worries. No chances. A seventy-year guarantee card. Is that what you want, Cathy?'

She half-smiled. 'Just at the moment it sounds a wonderful idea. All this raw emotion flying around – love, triangles, drug overdoses, it's knocking me out.'

He stared back at her belligerently, started to grin, and finally burst into loud, cracked laughter.

'It's like a crappy TV soap opera,' he said, irrepressibly.

He pulled her to him again, laughing and kissing her at the same time. 'Where's Chris? When do I get out of this place?'

'I don't think you can yet. I mean doesn't attempted suicide have to be reported to the police? And you have to see a psychiatrist.'

'You mean you get busted for trying to get *dead?* A suicide charge?' He began to laugh again. 'Hey, the Connection never had one of those before. Assault, drugs, debt, indecency, kidnap, paternity orders...but not suicide. Where's Chris. Fetch Chris in. He must hear this!'